The Little Girl's Treasury
of
Precious Things

Compiled by
Annie Brooks

Grace & Truth Books
Sand Springs, Oklahoma

ISBN# 1-58339-125-8
First printings, 1800's (date unknown)
Second printing, Triangle Press, 1996
Third printing, Grace & Truth Books, 2002

Cover design by Ben Gundersen

Grace & Truth Books
3406 Summit Boulevard
Sand Springs, Oklahoma   74063

Phone: 918 245 1500
www.graceandtruthbooks.com
email: gtbooksorders@cs.com

TABLE OF CONTENTS

Preface

This little book is a collection of short tales and stories, each gathered by a little girl – Annie Brooks – in her own reading. In the 19th century, Annie's family offered her collection to a publisher, in the hope that these favorites of hers might provide as much spiritual enrichment, for the good of others, as they had for Annie's own life and walk with God.

Feeling that she could not do much, yet anxious to do what she could, to glorify her Savior and to benefit the souls of others, she sought, in this humble way, to communicate some important truths to her young friends.

The Little Girl's Treasury of Precious Things

~ *Spare Moments* ~

Have you ever thought what might be done in the many "spare moments" of the day, which pass by unemployed, simply because, as you say, "It is not worthwhile to get anything to do?" Well, I will tell you a story of a little girl, who was quite useful, merely by filling up the corners of her time; her name was Annie Brooks.

Little Annie's mama once took her to a children's missionary meeting, where she listened very attentively to all that was said, especially when a missionary began to speak of the schools in India. He told them there were many poor little boys and girls in India, who were longing to go to school, but they could not pay the necessary sum of money and consequently were obliged to stay away. The missionary then asked the children at the meeting if they, who had so many kind friends to take care of them, and so many opportunities of learning, would not like to help these poor little heathen. He told them it only required fifteen dollars a year to educate, feed, clothe, in fact, entirely provide for a child in India; and that many of the little ones who were now enjoying the above advantages were supported by the contributions of children, and he entreated all present to try and aid this great work.

All this made a deep impression on little Annie, and she was very thoughtful going home, wondering what a little girl like her could do. Now Annie was very clever at crochet work, and she began to think whether, if she did some crochet work, she should be able to sell it; for the money could go to the education of one of those little Indians. But then she went to school every day, and when she came home, she had not much time for working. This thought troubled her, and she determined to ask her mama's advice on the subject. Mrs. Brooks was much pleased that her little girl was so anxious to be useful, and determined to aid her all she could. "'Tis true, my love," she said, "you have not much spare time now that you go to school; but suppose you were to make good use of what little you have, instead of spending it idly; for I think many a half hour slips by unawares which might be turned to good account. Now, for instance, how often are you downstairs in the morning some time before your papa, or me? What do you do then?"

"Oh, nothing, mama; it is never worthwhile to get anything out for that short time; for I am never waiting more than a quarter of an hour at the outside."

"Well, but, my child, supposing you wait a quarter of an hour for breakfast, the same for dinner, the same for tea and supper; that makes in the course of the day, a whole hour — *wasted*. How much you might have done in that time! Don't you remember the old proverb: 'Take care of the pence, and the pounds will take care of themselves?' May we not also say, 'Take care of the moments, and the hours will take care of themselves?' Then I will tell you another way in which you may save time. Instead of taking half an hour when you are going to dress for a walk, to put on your things, do you not think, if you were quick, you could do it in a quarter of an hour, and then, if you are ready before me, take out your crochet? That is just the thing for spare moments!"

Little Annie thought what her mama said very true, and determined to do what she could. Will you be surprised to learn that, merely by filling up the corners of her time, she had, by the end of the year, earned sufficient by the sale of her crochet, to place a little Indian child at school, to her great delight? Now all children may not be able to do so much as little Annie, for all, perhaps, do not work so quickly. But will all who read this true story think whether they have not hitherto wasted many an odd moment that might have been employed? And let us all try, henceforth, to gather up the *fragments* of our time, that *nothing* be lost.

~ *Love to Christ* ~

A little child, when dying, was asked where it was going. "To heaven," said the child.

"And what makes you wish to be there?" said one.

"Because Christ is there," replied the child.

"But," said a friend, "what if Christ should leave heaven?"

"Well," said the child, "I will go with him."

Some time before its departure, it expressed a desire to have a golden crown when it died. "And what will you do," said one, "with a golden crown?"

"I will take the crown, said the child, "and cast it at the feet of Christ."

Does not such a child, to use the language of prophecy, die a hundred years old?

~ *Weep With Those That Weep* ~

The cold winds whistled and whirled along the narrow streets in a perfect tempest of rudeness, defying the protection of cloaks and comforters, and causing large and small to shiver at its keen and searching roughness. Little Bettie Moore was standing by the window, wrapped to the chin in a large shawl, looking out into the street at the passersby. In the room behind her burned a large fire, and her little brother was rolling on the rug before it, very happy, in the enjoyment of comfortable idleness. "Oh, George," said Bettie, do come here; only see this old man, buttoned up to the chin, and wrapped to the eyes, blundering along against the wind. Now here comes a young lady trying to walk gracefully, but she cannot for pain. See, now she stoops forward, as if to let the blast drive over her head. Ha! ha!

"What next, Bettie?" said George. "I am too lazy to come and look; if you'll tell me, it will do just as well." And with this, he yawned, and stretched his feet toward the glowing fire.

"Oh, George, will you believe it? A man is coming with a little coffin in his arms! There, he has placed it on the stone step at the gate, and is looking so sad; I'll run down to the door, and ask him if I can do anything for him." Forgetting the cold, little Bettie ran down the stairs, and swinging open the front door rushed out to the gate.

The man glanced upward at her a moment, and then, dropping his head on the lid of the coffin, burst into an agony of tears. Little Bettie stooped down and wept also. What a scene! The little finely-clad child, and the rough, half-dressed man, weeping together over that small unvarnished coffin.

"God bless you, little miss; sure it must be that God has sent you to feel for the broken-hearted. May the spirit of God attend you, and shield you from evil."

"Is it your little girl?" asked Bettie.

"Yes."

"Well, you can meet her again if you'll repent. Mama says we'll meet our little buried sister in heaven if we love God, He gives us a new heart, and He brings us to the truth to do to others as we would have them do to us. Oh, I'm so sorry for you," she continued, almost choked with sobs, "but if you'll try, with the help of God, you can meet your little girl in heaven."

"I will, with God's help," said the man, looking at the child through his moistened lashes in astonishment. "Will you pray for me, little lady?"

"Yes, sir; I'll pray for you every night before I go to bed; and if you'll come to church on Sunday, you'll hear our good minister pray for you; he always prays for 'the sorrowing ones of earth.'"

"God bless you, little darling! I'll go to church, for your sake. Goodbye now! Run into the house; it's cold for the like of you;" and the man gathered up his child's coffin, and resumed his journey. Alas! alas! for friendless poverty, that must, unheeded and alone, bear its own loved to the yawning and repulsive grave! Yet, thank God that there are mothers who teach their children the way to heaven; that there are ministers who never forget to pray for the bereaved and afflicted. Yes, thank God that there are children who remember, and can repeat, the lessons taught them. The poor, sorrow-stricken man did go to church, the minister did pray for him, and he finally joined the church, and died at last in the hope of reunion with his lost babe.

~ Little Mary and the Old Woman ~

A happy, bright little girl is Mary P—, and I believe it is because she is always trying to do someone a kindness. I went one day to see a poor woman eighty-six years old, who lives by herself in a dark basement-room, and who depends entirely upon charity for her support. On my return, I was relating an account of my visit to Mary's mother. The little girl listened with great interest, and then said, "Oh mother, please let me carry her over some breakfast and dinner every day; we have so much left, much more than she could eat." The child had the matter so much at heart that her mother consented; and now you can see this little girl, after breakfast and after dinner each day, filling a basket with good and wholesome food for old Mrs. G—. Many a fine apple, peach, plum, and pear are slipped into the basket to refresh the poor woman's feeble appetite.

No matter how eager her little sisters are for Mary to play with them, no matter how hot the sun, or how heavily the rain pours down, little Mary never gets tired, and never forgets to provide the breakfast and dinner for the poor woman. Sometimes she takes the Bible and reads some beautiful chapters, for the poor woman is almost blind, and it comforts her much to hear the blessed word of life. Sometimes Mary takes her doll's frocks and sits down by her side, and sews a while, and chats away merrily to amuse her.

"She brings a ray of sunshine in with her every time she comes," said the poor woman with tears in her eyes, "which brightens up my dark room long after she has gone. She is one of Christ's own flock, I am sure."

Mary is but eight years old. Some of you have perhaps thought that you were not old enough yet to do anything for Christ and his poor. Is there no poor woman or hungry child to whom you can take the food which would never be missed from your plentiful store?

~ Faith in God ~

Late in the autumn of last year, a pale, quiet little girl came to my school, requesting to be admitted. She said that she had recently come from the country, and now lived in the district where the school was situated. Her dress indicated poverty, but there was a delicate cleanliness in her person and garments that, to an experienced eye, told of intelligent parents. Several months passed, and by her sweetness of disposition, her punctuality, and good scholarship, Ellen Brown had become very dear to me. I had often wished to learn something more of her circumstances, but the press of duties had put off my visit from time to time.

She was absent from school on a Monday morning. During the afternoon session I sent a little girl to her house to inquire if she was ill. The messenger reported that Ellen was well, but that Mrs. Brown was sick in bed and that Ellen would not come to school at present; and then with tears in her eyes, and a sudden grasp of my hand, the little girl said, "If you will only go and see them, I shall be so glad, for I know that they are very poor. There was no fire in the room, and it made me shiver to stay there."

I promised to go, while my heart smote me for my past negligence.

The early shade of a December night was settling upon the crowded streets, as I wended my way to this suffering family. The street was in a miserable locality, and the house was crowded with rough and vulgar, if not vicious people. Upon my reaching the door, my light rap was answered by Ellen, who seized my hand and almost ran with me to the opposite corner of the room, saying softly, when she reached the bed, "Mother, wake up and see my teacher, who has come to see us."

A small woman, apparently about thirty years of age, lay before me, but thin and pale. At the sound of her daughter's voice, a slight twitching of the eyelids was observable, and then the languid eyes opened, those eyes that would so soon close for the last time upon all earthly things.

She gazed in my face a moment, and then faintly said, "God is good. He never utterly forsakes those who put their trust in Him." The effort of uttering these words brought on a violent coughing fit, which, however, lasted but a few moments. After it was passed, I looked about the room. Besides the bed on which the invalid lay, there was only a table and one chair in the room, and over the fireplace an empty candlestick. I asked Ellen if they had a candle. She replied that there was a little piece that she had saved, so that she could strike a light if her mother should be very bad in the night. I bade her light it, and keep up courage a little while, till I returned.

It was the work of half an hour to order a small supply of fuel and food, leave word for a physician to call, obtain a little wine, and return. But soon a flame was dancing in the grate; Ellen was making a supper, and the invalid was somewhat refreshed. When the physician arrived, he confirmed my worst fears. Mrs. Brown saw it as well as I.

"Then you think, sir, that I can last but a little longer?"

"I fear it is so," he replied.

"It is well," were her softly uttered words, and the closed eyes, the clasped hands, the sweet expression, told us that she was conversing with God, and almost face to face. The veil of flesh was nearly rent in twain.

Dr. M. left only a cordial, and bade me watch carefully through the night. It was a happy privilege. Mrs. Brown's energies seemed to have revived. She did not sleep, and before morning she had told me her sad history. Not one complaint did she utter, not once did she betray any impatience, and when I inquired, as she finished her tale, if her courage had never faltered, if she could always put faith in God, her reply was, "Does He not provide for the ravens? Are not the hairs of our heads all numbered?" and then she continued, "I bless God that he has enabled me, through all my trials, to see his hand ever before me. Yes, even with regard to Ellen, I trust in him. He will temper the wind to the shorn lamb, though my poor wisdom cannot see the way he will take."

Her husband, who was a mechanic, had died, leaving only the household furniture. They had no friends to whom they could apply, and in their secluded home there was no work to be had that Mrs. Brown was strong enough to do. She sold her furniture, except what would furnish one little room, and came to the city, hoping to earn a living by doing fine sewing, at which she was very expert. But unacquainted with the city and with city customs, she had tried in vain to procure work of the kind she needed, and was obliged to take the very coarsest from one of the wholesale establishments. She could not earn enough for support without working almost all night, and her health failed at once. Piece by piece her furniture had been pawned, and till this very night no friendly face had crossed her threshold. She had kept Ellen at school as long as she dared, for the sake of the warmth of the schoolroom, and when I entered she was praying that some hand might be near to close her eyes at last.

Toward morning, she fell into a short slumber, and on awaking rose in bed, and called in a clear tone to Ellen. The child sprang up, and in a moment was folded in her mother's arms. In a clear voice, the mother said, "Trust in God, my child, always; He will never forsake you;" and fell back upon her pillow a corpse.

After the funeral was over, I took Ellen to stay with me a few days, till Dr. M and I could find a home for her; but she clung to me, and was so sweet and gentle in her grief, that I could not part with her. She has been my child since that sad night.

~ The Little French Girl ~

Two or three years back, some worthy peasants, becoming financially poor, were under the necessity of parting with their seven children; and they got those who were of sufficient age into service with the neighbouring farmers. Their greatest difficulty was in finding a suitable place for their youngest daughter, a girl of about ten years of age. At length, however, they heard of a respectable family, the heads of which were looking out for such an assistant in their household concerns. A few days before the girl left the parental roof, one of our peddlers called at the house, and was particularly struck with the seriousness with which she listened to what he said about the Scriptures. At her pressing entreaties, the father was prevailed upon to buy a New Testament for her. She took it with her on going to her new abode, with the avowed determination of making a daily use of it. She learnt that she must entreat the Lord for faith to believe in His word. She therefore prayed night and morning before beginning to read her book; nothing could withdraw her from this practice. To accomplish this, she was obliged to sit up later and get up earlier than the rest of the family; she had to bear the jokes of her fellow servants, older than herself. But nothing deterred her; and the Lord soon granted her all the blessing which such steadfastness always gains. She became a devout Christian. Her employers were at first struck with her good behaviour; no fault had they to find with the manner in which she performed the duties assigned to her. One thing alone displeased her mistress; she had declared that, from motives of conscience, no one could make her attend mass. The lady spoke of the matter to her husband, who, in his devotion, consulted his confessor on the subject — a Jesuit of great renown. A few days afterwards, the man in question, who was the religious director of persons only of the first rank, deigned to converse with the little maid. On learning that it was the reading of the New Testament which had plunged her into what he styled the most detestable heresy, he tried, at first, words of kindness; but finding them useless, he proceeded to the most terrible threats, with a view of inducing the little girl to deliver her book into his hands. But it was all labour lost; and the priest, after more than an hour's contest, went away defeated by the firmness of the little maid. He then, it seems, ordered the master and mistress to take the book from her, for, in his estimation, having made such bad a use of it.

The little girl watched with greater care than ever over her treasure, which some now sought to deprive her of. As her New Testament was one of the smallest size, it was easy for her always to have it about her without its being seen. At night her precious book was placed under her pillow; but her great care was to learn every day by heart a number of passages, so that if the attempt to deprive her of the word of God were successful, she might still possess some of its precious truths on which to meditate. It was well for her that she did this; for being betrayed by a fellow servant, her mistress, one night while she was soundly asleep, succeeded in laying hold of the New Testament, which the next day was forwarded in triumph to the Jesuit, to be by him committed to the flames. The sorrow of the little girl was intense, and it was only assuaged by the repetition of the consoling passages that she was able to recall to mind. It seemed to her, when repeating them to herself evening and morning at her devotions, that these passages affected her much more than when she had read them from her book.

Meanwhile, trials of various kinds came upon the family in whose service she was; monetary losses, and the death of beloved offspring, plunged the master and mistress of our young friend into mourning and tears. The afflicted ones, in the first instance, had recourse to their confessor; numerous masses were said, and an abundance of candles burnt; but alas! their sorrow remained as deep as ever and consolation they found not. The little servant did not look on with a dry eye; her heart sympathized with their afflictions; she implored, on behalf of her employers that comfort which proceeds alone from the Supreme Comforter. One evening when she thought herself secure from any disturbance, she, on bended knees, in her little chamber, offered up one of those petitions that are the genuine expression of the soul in behalf of those who were in sorrow and in tears. Her mistress, who had happened to pass the room, on hearing this supplicating voice, stopped, and, drawing near to the door, was deeply affected at hearing the prayer that was being offered up for herself and her husband. She related to him what had occurred; and the next morning both of them stationed themselves as listeners at the door of their little maid's room, who, being accustomed to pray aloud, commenced the same petitions as those of the preceding evening. Both went away deeply and seriously impressed, and with the desire of again hearing similar prayers. This desire led them, on different evenings, to the same place; and when their little maid expressed herself thus, "Thou hast said, Lord," followed by a passage; "Thou hast promised, O God," again followed by another passage — these declarations of Scripture were the portions of prayer which seemed to do them the most good; and they felt an ardent wish to become more intimately acquainted with them. This led them to inquire of the young girl, who it was that taught her the things that she mentioned in her prayer. "Who?" replied she; "the New Testament which you caused Father C— (the Jesuit) to take away from me." From that moment the employers and their little servant had frequent conversations respecting the New Testament. The former expressed increasing pleasure at listening to the recital of passages by the latter, by means of which God wrought a work of grace in their afflicted souls.

Matters were progressing thus, when one day some person rang the doorbell, and, on the young servant going to and answering it, whom does she behold? — a dealer of the same description as the one who had supplied her with her New Testament. On seeing him, she uttered an exclamation of joy, so loud that her master ran to the spot; and, on being informed, he asked the dealer to step into his room. His wife was called in also, after which a long conversation took place, which ended in the buying of a Bible for the use of the master and mistress, and of a New Testament, which they presented to the little girl. I will only add, that at the present time the master and mistress, and the little servant maid, are true and eager disciples of the Word, who have gathered around them several individuals, of some of whom it may be said that they are very near to the kingdom of heaven; a matter which deeply afflicts the Jesuit. "It would be shameful," he continued to say to his former flock, "for your little servant to gain the victory; for ignorance to show itself more powerful than science; for darkness to win over light." "No, no," was the reply; "this little girl is but a feeble instrument. What has made a change in us, and what has taught us, is the Word of God — the candle which you hide; against this you can accomplish nothing."

~ *Going Home* ~

"I'm going home," was the reply of a bright-eyed young girl to an acquaintance as they were boarding the train. The thought seemed to light up her lovely face with sunbeams of additional loveliness as she uttered the words.

"I'm going home to cheer my father amid the perplexities of business; to support my mother in the downhill journey of life; to rescue, by my loving advice, a brother from the devious paths of error and vice; to point my young sister to the bright path of virtue and usefulness, and to lead the way myself by my example." What noble thoughts were in the mind of this young girl!

"I'm going home!" was a delightful thought to contemplate. Within the loving circle of her family were joys that the world's allurements could not replace. Her face radiated the joy as the following scene rose to her imagination: Smiles, appearing the more lovely because the faces that had beamed with them were furrowed with wrinkles — smiles are more touching, for shining through tearful eyes — a welcome that came from the treasure-house of their hearts. Her anticipation and gladness were reflected in her smiling countenance and crystal clear eyes.

"I'm going home!" Alas! Many cannot utter that cheering thought with her. To some, home is but the furnace of trial and affliction; an escape from it even for a moment is like the green oasis in the burning desert of life. Going to such a home of trial is a return to prison, chains, torture, and a life-long death. Courage, brave heart! The furnace purifies while it tries; the torture strengthens while it humbles; the prison has blessings amid its gloom. Even the necessity and duty of such a character going to such a home will face a dismal wall and instruments of torture. Work on, then, brave heart! The home may yet be made a paradise by your efforts and become a blessing that can be found nowhere else this side of the great home of heaven!

"I'm going home!" There are some who can never utter that exclamation. There are those who are young and tender, and beautiful, too, to whom the word "home" is unknown. They have no earthly refuge where love can meet them with its joys or sacred pleasures, or the family fill their affections. Let such have the sympathy they need, with all the assistance that the virtuous can give to support their steps and draw them away from vice.

"I'm going home!" — sometimes the last words we hear from a departing soul. Earth, with all its rational joys, is not our home. The properly disciplined heart knows that earth is but a pilgrimage — a journey that must soon terminate. Such a heart rejoices that there is a permanent home made happy by the presence of the Infinite. It is, therefore, with a smile on the cheek of the departing, lovelier than that of the returning maiden, and with a heavenly brightness of eye far outshining hers, that he exclaims, "I'm going home!"

~ I Forgot to Pray ~

"Don't touch my books, Eddy," said little Sarah Wilcox, in a peevish tone of voice. "Don't touch them at all. I piled them up just as I want them to stay.

"I am afraid my little daughter does not feel quite pleasant this morning," said a pale, but sweet-faced lady, who sat in an easy chair near the stove. "Come to me, Sarah, and let me ask you a question."

The little girl slowly approached her mother, who put her arm around her, and in a low tone of voice asked her if she had prayed to God, and asked him to make her kind and pleasant through the day.

"No, mother," said the little girl, "I forgot to pray."

"Forgot to pray, Sarah! I am very sorry; you have then forgotten to thank God for keeping you alive and well through the night. You have forgotten God, I fear, entirely; but I see that he has not forgotten you."

"How do you say that he has not forgotten me, mother?" said the child, looking up, as if half surprised, in the lady's face.

"Why, I see that he is watching over you and taking care of you every minute now. If he should forget or neglect you, your lips would cease to open; you could not move your hands or feet; you could not hear or see, and your little form would become cold and stiff in death."

Sarah looked very serious while her mother was thus speaking, and when she had finished, she said, "Pray for me, dear mother. Pray to God to forgive me for forgetting to thank him, and ask him to make me a good girl all the day."

"I will, my dear; but you must pray for yourself. I would go up into your little room now if I were you, and offer up a simple prayer to your kind and heavenly Father."

So Sarah left the room, to follow her mother's directions.

~ *Too Poor to Pay* ~

Yes, it was a lovely spot, that village graveyard! Such a one, I fancy, as inspired the "Elegy in a country church-yard." There was less pomp and show than in our only burial places, but what of that? — as Jeremy Taylor says, "We cannot deceive God and nature, for a coffin is a coffin, thought it be covered with a sumptuous pall." So a grave is a grave, though it be piled over with sculptured marble.

Then that little girl! How her image comes up before me, bending over her brother's grave! I marked her when she entered, and was soon drawn toward the spot where she was kneeling. I approached cautiously — there was something so sacred in my thoughts of a child weeping at a new-made grave, that I feared my presence might interrupt her mournful musings. I know not how long I might have stood, apparently reading the rude gravestone, had not the child raised her eyes and timidly said:

"Our little Willie sleeps here! We're too poor to get a tombstone; we and the angels know where he lies, and mother says that's enough."

"Are you not afraid to be here alone?" I asked.

"Oh no; mother is sick and couldn't come, so she said I must come and see if the violets were in bloom yet."

"How old was your brother? I asked, feeling interested in the little girl.

"He was only seven years old; and he was so good, and he had such beautiful eyes; but he couldn't see a bit!"

"Indeed! Was he blind?"

"You see, he was sick a long time; yet his eyes were blue and bright as blue skies with stars in them, and we did not know he was getting blind, till one day I brought him a pretty rose, and he asked, 'Is it a white rose, Dora?'"

"'Can't you see, darling?' asked mother.

"'No, I can't see anything. I wish you would open the window, it is so dark.'

"Then we knew that the poor little Willie was blind; but he lived a long time after that, and used to put his dear little hand on our faces to feel if we were crying, and tell us not to cry, for he could see God and heaven and the angels. 'Then never mind, mother and Dora,' he'd say, 'I'll see you, too, when you go away from this dark place.'

"So one day he closed his eyes and fell asleep, and mother said he was asleep in Jesus. Then we brought him here and buried him; and though we're too poor to get a tombstone, yet we can plant flowers on his little grave, and nobody shall trouble them, I know, when they learn that our little Willie sleeps here."

~ Little Allie ~

Mama, when will it be spring?" said Althea C—, earnestly. She was almost three years old, and I had never seen a more beautiful child; her cheeks and lips full and red with health, her blue eyes kindling with excitement, and her little form so plump and round, that when I lifted her to my knees she said, "I'm fat as butter."

"Why are you so anxious that it should be spring, dear?" said I, supposing that it was for the sunshine, birds, and flowers.

"Allie will go to church in the spring," was her reply.

"Why does Allie wish to go to church?"

"God is there," she replied solemnly."

"Do you love God, Althea?"

"Oh, very, very much."

"To-morrow will be spring, darling." And she ran away singing, "To-morrow, to-morrow; I shall be so happy to-morrow." But she was not quite satisfied. In a few minutes she returned, saying, "Mama, can I go to church to-morrow, and hear them pray and sing and preach?"

"No, my dear, tomorrow is Wednesday; it will be three days before the Sabbath."

An expression of disappointment clouded her sweet face; but when told that three days would pass quickly, and that God made the days, she seemed satisfied.

Some time during the night, Mrs. C— sent to me in haste that Althea was dying. Scarcely taking time to thank the one who informed me, I rushed to the house, but she was a corpse. Her mother told me that several times after I left her, as if forgetful of a part of the conversation, she was singing, "To-morrow, to-morrow; I shall be so happy to-morrow." Each time, when corrected, she seemed to dismiss the subject; but she had been longing for spring, that she might go to the house of God, and she could not at once give up the idea that with the first day would commence her pleasure. Just before sunset she complained of extreme weariness, and soon dropped to sleep. When she awoke she was burning with fever, and her father went for a physician. During his absence she became delirious, and when the physician approached the bedside, he turned away sadly, saying, "Madam, it is too late." Another physician was summoned, and another, and a fourth even, but all of no avail. Her disease was scarlet brain fever, and in eleven hours from her first complaining, her spirit had passed away. We buried her on the morrow, a balmy, lovely day — the first of spring. And when the earth rang on the coffin-lid, her words breathed in our sorrowing hearts, "To-morrow, to-morrow; I shall be so happy to-morrow." Precious one! We hope she has joined the Assembly and Church of the First-born on high.

~ *Love One Another* ~

As little Annie and her brother Frank were playing in the nursery, Annie accidentally struck her brother with a ball; and he ran to his mother and told her that she had hurt him, and was a bad girl, and ought to be punished.

Then Annie came with tearful eyes, and said, "Show me where I hurt you, and I will kiss it and make it well." But he would not hear her; so she turned away that she might give vent to her tears, for her little heart was wronged and wounded indeed.

Frank did not come into the room all that day. When evening came his mother said, Go, find your sister, and come and get your supper." Then he ran up to the nursery, but she was not there; then he went to the little brook, and there, beneath the shade of the spreading foliage, upon a mossy bank, lay little Annie sleeping, and on her cheek was a bright tear. But he could not speak to her, for his heart grew sad and the tears started from his eyes; so he stole thoughtfully back to the house.

The next morning Frank's mother called him to her, and told him Annie was quite ill and he must not make a noise. As each day rolled on she grew worse, and after a few mornings more his mother took him to her room alone, where all was quiet save the sweet notes of the early birds. There with the bitter anguish of her heart she told him his dear sister was dead. Oh, how he wept, and wept again! How he longed that he might kiss that tear from off her cheek! Alas! it was too late. Never again would those little dimpled arms be thrown around his neck. Her warm lips would press his cheek no more forever. And then when the dark night came, and he was taken to his bed, he cried and sobbed aloud, and tossed upon his pillow, for he seemed to hear a sweet-toned voice whispering, "Show me where I hurt you, and I will kiss it and make it well." Dear children, be ever ready to forgive. Be kind to each other. Love your brothers and sisters. Let us hear what God says: "He that loveth not his brother, abideth in death." "Whoso hateth his brother is a murderer." Never forget that God has commanded, "Little children, love one another."

~ The Tiger Story ~

Lucy and Fanny were two little girls who lived with their father and mother in London. When Lucy was six and Fanny was five years old, their uncle George came home from India. This was a great joy to them; he was so kind, and had so much to tell them about far away places, and strange people, and animals, and things such as they had never seen. They never wearied of hearing his stories, and he did not seem to weary either at telling them.

One day after dinner, they both climbed on his knees, and Lucy said, "O Uncle, do tell us a *tiger* story."

"Very well," he said; "I will tell you a story about a tiger and a baby, which happened to some friends of my own. This gentleman and his lady had one sweet little baby, and they had to take a long journey with it through a wild part of India. There were no houses there, and they had to sleep in a tent. That is a kind of a house made of cloth by driving high sticks firmly into the ground, and then drawing curtains all over them. It is very comfortable and cool in a warm country where there is no rain; but then there are no doors or windows to shut as we do at night, to make all safe. One night they had to sleep in a very wild place, near a thick wood. The lady said,

"'Oh, I feel so afraid to-night; I cannot tell you how frightened I am. I know there are many tigers and wild animals in the wood; and what if they should come out upon us?'

"Her husband replied, 'My dear, we will make the servants light a fire, and keep watch, and you need have no fear; and we must put our trust in God.'

"So the lady kissed her baby and put it into its cradle; and then she and her husband knelt down together, and prayed to God to keep them from every danger, and they repeated that pretty verse, *I will both lay me down in peace, and sleep; for thou, Lord only makest me dwell in safety.*

"In the middle of the night the lady started up with a loud cry, 'Oh, my baby! my baby! I dreamed just now that a great tiger had crept below the curtains and ran away with my child!'

"And when she looked into the cradle, the baby was not there! Oh, you may think how dreadful was their distress! They ran out of the tent, and there in the moonlight they saw a great animal moving toward the wood, with something white in his mouth. They wakened all the servants, and got loaded guns, and all went after it into the wood. They went as fast, and yet quietly, as they could, and very soon they came to a place where they saw through the trees that the tiger had lain down and was playing with the baby, just as pussy does with a mouse before she kills it. The poor father and mother could only pray to the Lord for help, and when one of the men took up his gun, the lady cried, 'Oh, you will kill my child!'

"But the man raised the gun and fired once, and God made him do it well. The tiger gave a loud howl, and jumped up, and then fell down again, shot quite dead. Then they all rushed forward, and there was the dear baby quite safe and smiling as if it were not at all afraid."

"And did the baby really live?"

"Yes, the poor lady was very ill afterwards, but the baby not at all. I have seen it often since then. You may be sure that often, when they looked at the child afterwards, the parents gave thanks to God. It was he who made the mother dream, and awake just at the right minute, and made the tiger hold the baby by the clothes so as not to hurt it, and the man fire so as to shoot the tiger and not the child. But now good night, my dear little girls; and before you go to bed, pray to God to keep you safe, as my friend did that night in the tent."

~ Mother Knows Best ~

A party of little girls stood talking beneath my window. Some nice plan was afoot; they were going into the woods, and they meant to make oakleaf trimming, and pick berries, and carry luncheons. Oh, it was a fine time they meant to have! "Now," said they to one of their number, "Ellen, you run home and ask your mother if you may go. Tell her we are all going, and you must." Ellen, with her green cape bonnet, skipped across the way and went into the house opposite. She was gone for some time.

The little girls kept looking up to the windows very impatiently. At length the door opened, and Ellen came down the steps. She did not seem to be in a hurry to join her companions, and they cried out, "Have you got leave? You are going, are you?" Ellen shook her head, and said that her mother could not let her go.

"Oh," cried the children, "it is too bad! Not go! It is really unkind of your mother."

"Why, I would *make* her let you."

"Oh! Oh!"

"I would go whether or no."

"My mother knows best," was Ellen's answer, and it was a beautiful one. Her lip quivered a very little, for I suppose she wanted to go, and was much disappointed not to get leave; but she did not look angry or pouting, and her voice was very gentle, but firm, when she said, "My mother knows best." There are a great many occasions when mothers do not see fit to give their children leave to go where and do what they wish to; and how often are they rebellious and pouting as a result! But this is not the true way, for it is not pleasing to God.

The true way is cheerful obedience in your mother's decision. Trust her, and smooth down your ruffled feelings by the sweet and beautiful thought. "My mother knows best." It will save you many tears and much sorrow. It is the gratitude you owe her, who has done and suffered so much for you.

~ Little Lucy and Her Song ~

A little child six summers old,
So thoughtful and so fair,
There seemed about her pleasant ways
A more than childish air,
Was sitting on a summer eve
Beneath a spreading tree,
Intent upon an ancient book,
Which lay upon her knee.

She turned each page with careful hand,
And strained her sight to see,
Until the drowsy shadows slept
Upon the grassy lea;
Then closed the book, and upward looked,
And straight began to sing
A simple verse of hopeful love –
This very childish thing:

"While here below, how sweet to know
His wondrous love and story,
And then, through grace, to see his face,
And live with him in glory!"

That little child, one dreary night
Of winter wind and storm,
Was tossing on a weary couch
Her weak and wasted form;
And in her pain, and in its pause,
But clasped her hands in prayer –
(Strange that we had no thoughts of heaven,
While hers were only there) –

Until she said, "O mother dear,
How sad you seem to be!
Have you forgotten that He said
'Let children come to Me?'

Dear mother, bring the blessed Book,
Come mother, let us sing;"
And then again, with faltering tongue,
She sang that childish thing:

"While here below, how sweet to know
His wondrous love and story,
And then, through grace, to see His face,
And live with him in glory!"

Underneath a spreading tree
A narrow mound is seen,
Which first was covered by the snow,
Then blossomed into green;
Here first I heard that childish voice
That sings on earth no more;
In heaven it hath a richer tone,
And sweeter than before:

For those who know His love below –
So runs the wondrous story –
In heaven, through grace, shall see his face,
And dwell with him in glory!

~ Little Deeds of Kindness ~

That old man, how often have I watched him as he totters slowly up the aisle of the village church to his accustomed seat, the seat he has occupied for more than three-score years! His form is bent with age, and his thin locks are white with the frosts of many winters. His hat, time-worn like himself, which he has reverently laid aside before entering the church of God, he carefully places by his side. His coat, warm and comfortable, though not cut according to the style of the present season, is in my opinion far more becoming than any other could be, for he has worn it ever since my earliest remembrance.

He gazes not idly around him, but as the man of God rises to read the hymn for the opening service, he slowly draws forth his heavy silver-bound spectacles, and having carefully adjusted them, finds the place in his hymn book, and intently follows the minister from the beginning to the close of the hymn. The singing then absorbs his attention, while he again follows line by line as earnestly as before. The old man seems to take peculiar delight in this portion of divine service, and I doubt not, it has been his custom from earliest childhood, thus to participate. With the same attention, he carefully notes the text, and it requires but a small stretch of the imagination to see him, after his return home, before partaking of his frugal Sunday meal, take down the old family Bible, and finding the text, read it aloud to his wife and family — a good old custom, fast passing away.

But this morning, the tolling of the bell had ceased, the last note of the simple organ voluntary had died away — already the minister had arisen to give out the hymn, and yet my friend's seat was vacant.

Ah, thought I, something serious must have happened, for no trifling obstacle could prevent my old friend's attendance at public worship on God's holy day. But hark! a well-known step announces his approach! —a presence which, I doubt not, brings pleasure to other hearts as well as my own. Noiselessly he takes his seat, and at once gives his attention to the hymn. His hymn-book lies unopened, for he knows not the number, and of course cannot find it. I could not but regret sincerely his inability to follow the pastor, as was his wish, and desired that it were in my power to minister to his necessity.

Behind him sits a little girl, to whom finding the hymn is yet a novelty, as is seen by the interest and eagerness she manifests. She lifts her eyes from the open page, and her attention is arrested by that old man. She too notices the change. "And shall I give him my book?" her face seems to say. A flush over-spreads her features as she hesitates, fearing to attract attention; but a second glance at that eager, upturned face decides the question. She extends to him her hymn-book, pointing with her finger to the place. Pleasure and gratitude light up the countenance of the old man, and that little one is more than repaid for her gift.

But I hear my little reader say, "What a little thing!" It was indeed a little thing, almost as trifling a deed as giving a cup of cold water to a disciple, which you will remember our dear Saviour has said shall not lose its reward. But, little children, if you would do good, if you would be useful in the world, and contribute your share toward making others happy, you must watch for these *little* opportunities. Wealth and power may be denied you —but kind words and deeds, never. Use them ever so freely and they will not fail, but their good influence will reflect back into your own heart. A kind word or look often requires a greater struggle, more forgetfulness of self, than might be required for the gift of thousands from the man of wealth. But Jesus, in whose eye the gift of two mites was greater than all the other gifts cast into the treasury, will regard it, and you shall not lose your reward.

~ Little Mattie ~

"When can I read my title clear,
  To mansions in the skies,"
sang a sweet, childish voice. I looked within. My little house-maid was busy with the brush and the dustpan, her curly pate bobbing up and down as she went the rounds of her daily task.

Mattie was a bright-eyed, happy creature, always singing the good evangelical hymns of the olden time: and I had boasted to my friends of my treasure, till they had almost envied me the possession of the honest little serving-maid; and I went upstairs to my toilet, with her gentle music sounding in my ear, and thanked God that I too could sing, in the language of faith,

"I'll bid farewell to every fear,
And wipe my weeping eyes."

The blinds were all closed to shut out the hot sun. A soft and agreeable dimness pervaded the large, old-fashioned room, and a faint ruby tinge glowed through the heavy crimson curtains. Seated in an easy chair, I was reading sleepily, and the words were just blending into the strange prismatic confusion which precedes unconsciousness, when I heard a light step trip by, and almost without thought I found myself following a little form up the stairs.

In my boudoir stood Mattie looking at and handling a small diamond brooch, which I had often observed her gaze at with childish admiration. Evidently some struggle was going on in her hitherto innocent mind. She placed it down, lifted it again, held it at arm's length, and finally — Oh, how my heart sank! — she cast a hurried glance about her, concealed the brooch in her bosom, and then guiltily took up her simple sewing; she had always sat there to sew in the afternoon.

At first I felt like confronting her, for my temper is quick, but better thoughts prevailed. I returned to the sitting-room, and in a little time sent for Mattie.

She came slowly — her innocence was gone! The vivacious sparkle of her eye had faded, and without intending it, she assumed a side-long position.

"I am lonely, Mattie; bring your sewing here, sit on this little stool, and keep my company. You were singing a sweet hymn when I came down this morning, Mattie; who taught you to sing?"

"My mother, ma'am," came in a low, faint voice.

"Yes, I remember your mother, she was a sweet woman, a good Christian, and is now an angel. I don't believe she would willingly have done a wrong deed; do you, Mattie?"

"No, ma'am," murmured the child, and her cheeks crimsoned painfully.

"I remember," I went on, as if to myself, "how very beautiful she looked as she lay wasting away, and how quiet and happy she was when she came to die. Ah! Mattie, may you and I have just as sweet a dying pillow, may we never do anything wrong, and obey God's commandments."

I saw the flush deepening, the lips beginning to quiver. The little fingers shook violently as they passed the tremulous needle through; the little bosom heaved; I had touched the right chord.

"Mattie, I love to hear you sing; sing me that sweet hymn, beginning,

'Alas! and did my Saviour bleed.'"

The poor conscience-stricken little creature obeyed my request with a faltering voice. She conquered the first verse, but when she began on the second,

"Was it for crimes that I" –

her voice failed her, her frame quivered all over, and she burst into a passion of grief, burying her face in my lap.

Tears were running in swift streams down my own cheeks, as the heavy sobs told her suffering.

"Mattie," I said, as well as I was able to for emotion, "what have you been doing, my child, to make you weep thus?"

She dashed the guilt out of her bosom with the brooch, and throwing it wildly from her, sobbed, "I took it — I stole it! — I meant to sell it — Oh—!" and her prolonged moan was anguish itself.

I took the struggling child to my heart; I laid my hand upon her burning temples, and let her hide the wet, shame-covered face in my bosom. God knows I felt fully at that moment something of the divine nature of forgiveness, and the compassionate pity for sin, yet love for the sinner, which Christ is in perfection. In my mind's eye I saw a long and sorrowful procession of transgressors, headed by Mary Magdalene, forgiven and sanctified by our Saviour, and my prayer was, "Forgive us our trespasses, as we forgive those who trespass against us!"

~ *The Street Sweeper* ~

A gentleman was crossing one of our streets where a little girl was sweeping off the mud. Her little hand opened as he passed, and he hastily placed a penny — as he supposed! — therein. She immediately followed him, calling, "Sir! See what you have given me." The gentleman stopped, and she handed him an eagle, saying she did not think he meant to give her more than a penny. He asked why she did not keep it. She replied, "That would not have been right." He looked at her with astonishment, and inquired of whom she learned that. "In the Sunday-school," was her reply. He then inquired her name, age, and residence. Her mother, she said, was very poor, and lived in an obscure place. While he was talking with her, some fifteen or twenty persons were gathered around them, and a contribution was proposed, which resulted in the sum of about fifteen dollars. The gentleman called to see the little girl and her mother, and finding the statement he received verified, placed the mother in a tenement of his own, free of rent, and has taken the little girl to educate.

~ *Mary's Thanksgiving* ~

"Three cheers for Thanksgiving!" cried a rosy-cheeked boy, as he tossed his cap high in the air, and raised his voice still higher.

"*Six* cheers for Thanksgiving!" echoed his companions, who, being just let loose from school, could shout with hearty goodwill.

"Poor Tom Harris will have no Thanksgiving this year!" said one of their number, after they seemed fairly tired of their own noise.

"*Can't* he have any?"

"No; the Doctor says he won't be able to walk for a week; his ankle is hurt."

"Ain't you sorry you went on that excursion? I told you something would happen for going without leave."

"I'm sorry Tom got hurt," was the answer.

"So am I. Poor fellow! We must all go and see him tomorrow, and try to cheer him up."

"Yes, so we must; let's go now and tell him what fun we are going to have skating."

"Oh, I can't now. I must go and get my skates ready for tomorrow afternoon."

"And I must fix mine, too, but we must try and get time to go and see poor Tom."

"Yes, we will," was the resolution of each one, as he hurried home to prepare skates and other things which would be needed in carrying out their plans for enjoying the afternoon of the next day. Amid these absorbing occupations, I am sorry to say that none of them found time to visit their lame schoolmate, though they *did* think of him enough to repeat to each other, "Poor Tom has no Thanksgiving!"

Many bright faces were gathered in the parlor at the house of Tom's grandparents, and conversation was cheerful and animated. The choicest delicacies that the market afforded were being prepared in the kitchen, while the side-tables in the ample dining-room were loaded with such an array of choice fruits and confections as gladdened the hearts of the young people, who, with the privilege they always enjoyed "at grandma's," made a frequent visit to that important part of the house, just to see how things were going on.

But there was one young girl amid that merry company who cared for none of these things. The liveliest fun did not win a smile from her, for her thoughts were with her brother. Sweet Mary Harris! She could not bear the thought of leaving him all alone, *on Thanksgiving day, too*, and had begged to stay with him. But her parents said, "No, he deserved the punishment for his disobedience, and he must bear it alone." Mary dared not urge the matter any further; but not even the sight of the beautiful new dress her mother had prepared for the occasion, could reconcile her to the idea of going when Tom had to stay at home. And now she sat there, unable to think of anything but how sad and lonely poor Tom must feel. She had collected all her prettiest books, and laid them on the table by him; she had slipped under his handkerchief an orange that her uncle had given her, and had brought out the greatest treasure that she possessed — her box of paints — and welcomed him to amuse himself with it. Though he had not thanked her for these little attentions, and had even looked cross, and said pettishly, "Pshaw, I don't care about them!" and "I don't want any one to stay at home with me — I can take care of myself, I guess;" she only thought, "Poor fellow, how unhappy he has made himself by disobeying father!"

"Is Mary sick today?" asked grandma, coming up to the silent girl.

"No, Grandma; but I feel so sorry that poor brother Tom can have no Thanksgiving!"

"Well, I am very sorry, too; but you must not let it prevent you from enjoying yourself."

"Oh, I wish mother would let me go home to him! Do ask her to, won't you?"

"You must not go till after dinner," was the answer.

As the company was moving to the dining-room, Mary drew her mother aside and said pleadingly, "Mother, do let me go home to Tom. I don't want anything to eat; please let me go!" The mother was touched by the earnestness of her tones and the tears that trembled on her long lashes, and answered more kindly than she had done in the morning, "You may go as soon as you have had your dinner."

That dinner hour seemed very *long* to Mary, and as soon as she could, she made her escape from the company, and bidding grandma good-bye, ran up stairs for her bonnet and cloak. While she was putting them on, grandma was not idle, and as she was passing out of the hall, called her to take charge of a basket of nice things for Tom. Mary was so glad that she had thought of that; and as she thanked grandma for her kindness, the old lady said, "Tell Tom he must be a good boy, and not disobey his parents anymore, since he not only makes himself, but his sister, unhappy by doing so."

"I wonder if Tom will be glad to see me!" thought Mary, as her feet flew over the pavement. "I guess he will, though, for he must have been so lonely all the morning!"

He had indeed been lonely; and his "Why, Mary what brought you back so soon?" was uttered in a more pleasant tone than the usual. But when Mary sat down by him, and began to tell him how she had missed him, and could not enjoy anything because he was not there; and, spreading all the nice things before him, urged him to eat, he burst into tears — boy though he was — and said, "Mary, I don't deserve your kindness. I would not have been so cross to you this morning, but father and mother had both been scolding me, and telling me I was so wicked, and you were so much better than I, that it made me hate you for a little while."

"Never mind, Tom; eat some of those nice grapes, and tell me how you passed your time."

"I can't eat anything now, Mary; but I will tell you what I have been doing. I couldn't tell anyone else, though; I've been thinking that all father and mother ever tell me about my being so wicked, is true. I began to feel that I am the greatest sinner that ever lived, and that I don't deserve any mercy."

"Do you really feel so, Tom? I am so glad!"

"Glad, Mary?"

"Yes, for we are just in the right state to ask for mercy, when we feel that we don't deserve it. I felt just so once; it seemed to me that God ought to send me straight to hell for my wickedness; and then I just began to understand what a good thing it is to have a Saviour to go to — one who has died for us that he might take away our sins. I never knew before how much we need him."

"What did you do then, Mary?"

"I prayed to him as hard as I could pray; and I think he heard me and took away my bad heart, for I have felt so differently ever since!"

"How different?"

"Oh, I have loved him so much more; and liked to read about him in the Bible, and to hear of him in church; and I am so much more afraid to do wrong than I used to be — not because I shall get punished for it —but because I am afraid the Saviour will be grieved at it."

"Mary," said Tom, after a pause, "I wish you would pray with me; I've been trying to pray today, but I don't know how."

"O Tom, I never prayed out loud, and I don't know how to pray before anybody else."

"But you will pray for me now, that's a good sister. You don't know how unhappy I am, or you would not mind doing it."

"Well, I will try." And the young girl knelt, and reverently closing her eyes, prayed earnestly that the Saviour would give her brother a new heart. Tom listened with more interest than he could have done to the prayer of anyone else; and his heart was so softened that when she stopped, he began to pray, too. And the gracious Saviour heard the pleadings of those two children, and granted them the blessing which they asked.

That was the happiest evening of Tom's whole life. When his father and mother came home, they were surprised to see him looking so cheerful, and when he told them what he and Mary had done, and asked them to forgive him for all his past disobedience, they said that was the best Thanksgiving night they had ever known.

Tom always loves to think of that time, and often tells Mary that the day on which he expected to have no Thanksgiving was the very one on which he received the greatest blessing that anyone can have. A blessing for which he hopes to return thanks, not only as long as he lives here, but through all eternity.

~ The Forget-Me-Not ~

"Grandmother," said little Gretchen, "why do you call this beautiful flower, blue as the sky, growing by this brook, 'forget-me-not?'"

"My child," said the grandmother, I accompanied once your father, who was going on a long journey, to this brook. He told me when I saw this little flower, I must think of him and so we have always called it the 'forget-me-not.'"

Said happy little Gretchen, "I have neither parents, nor sisters, nor friends, from whom I am parted. I do not know whom I can think of when I see the 'forget-me-not.'"

"I will tell you," said her grandmother, "someone of whom this flower may remind you — Him who made it. Every flower in the meadow says, 'Remember God;' every flower in the garden and the field says to us of its Creator, 'Forget-me-not.'"

~ The Holiday ~

"O mother dear, I'm very tired;"
Said little Annie Gray;
"I wish I might remain at home,
And spend my time in play.
Instead of going off to school,
Through sun and rainy weather;
I would, if I could have my choice,
Stay with you altogether."

"Why, Annie, child, I am surprised
To hear you reason so;
You certainly would like to learn
What other people know.
But as you are not satisfied
With present times of leisure,
Tomorrow you may stay at home,
If it will give you pleasure."

Then Annie ran about with glee,
And shook her curly head;
And, laughing, ran to tell papa,
What dear mama had said.
"I'll bid good-bye to school," said she,
"And books that cause me sorrow;
For I have nothing else to do
But play all day tomorrow."

The morning came both bright and clear,
And Annie jumped from bed;
But anxious to begin her play,
She left her prayers unsaid.
And thus forgot that every day
Must have a good beginning—
That we must not neglect to pray
For grace to keep from sinning.

At first she hunted master Tray,
But he had broken loose,
And then had scampered far away;
So Annie sought for puss.
But pussy had not breakfasted,
And was intent on catching
A little mouse that tarried near,
Which she had long been watching.

She then went down into the yard,
Then to the garden plot;
Then took her bonnet off, and chased
The butterflies about;
But soon grew tired of doing this,
And ran to ask her mother,
If she might to the nursery go,
And hold her little brother.

Then Annie to the nursery hied,
But baby was in bed;
And he must have his daily nap,
The careful Margaret said.
So Annie slowly walked away,
Feeling quite sad and weary;
To stay at home and play alone,
She thought it rather dreary.

Again she to her mother went,
And sitting by her side,
Said, "Dear mama, I'm tired of play,
And all else that I've tried.
Although this day has been my own,
It only brought me sorrow;
So if you please, I'll get my books,
And go to school tomorrow."

"You'll always find it best, my child,
To do the thing that's right;
Duty neglected will not bring
True pleasure to our sight.
In this you feel that you have erred,
And precious time been wasting;
I hope this lesson that you've learned,
Will useful prove, and lasting."

~ The Sleepless Night ~

"I wish the clock would not tick so loud; I don't see why I can't get asleep," said Ruth Beach half aloud, as she tossed and tumbled about her bed, doubling up her pillow one moment to make it higher, and then throwing it aside, in her vain efforts to find an easy position. "I'm sure I didn't steal; I've done no harm." She generally dropped asleep soon after lying down, and slept so soundly, that if she chanced to wake when her father and mother retired to the next room, it seemed like morning. But now, she had listened to the footsteps of her brothers and sisters, as they went to their rooms, had heard her father wind up the old clock in the hall, and her mother's voice hushing the baby; all was still in the house except the ever-ticking clock, and yet she could not sleep.

Shall I tell you what troubled the little girl, so that the sound of the good old clock, whose face she had looked up to from infancy, was so distressing to her ears?

Ruth had been committing a very great sin. The little boy who sat next to her in school had a couple of new storybooks, which he was refusing to show her. She had looked at the beautiful blue covers and bright gilding many times, and wondering what was between them, and what the pictures were about, till she broke the *tenth commandment*, and *coveted* her neighbor's goods. After the children went home, and the teacher had locked the school-house door, and passed out of sight, Ruth lingered talking with Kitty Waters, a lively romping girl who feared no one. Ruth was urging Kitty to climb in the back window with her. "I'd just as soon do it as not," said Kitty, "but what do you want?"

"I'll show you when we are in," said Ruth; and raising the window, she helped Kitty, and climbed in after her. Ruth then led the way to Charley's desk, and opening it, said, "Look, Kitty, I want one of those books! Now, you can take it, and give it to me, and we can both say, '*I* didn't do it,' when the teacher finds it out and makes a fuss about it."

Kitty stood a moment, as if not comprehending Ruth's meaning, and then touching the gilded letters with her fore-finger, she stooped and read the titles; and said, "Now, Ruth if you wanted to play a trick on Charley,

I'd like the fun of hiding one of them a little while; but I dare not steal, for the world."

"No one would ever know it, Kitty, and we would have fine times reading in our barn after school; besides, Charley is so mean, he deserves to lose his books."

"O Ruth," said Kitty, as she looked with a shudder around the empty school-room, "God will know it. It scares me to think of being a thief. Do let us go out again."

Ruth shut the desk, after giving the books another longing look; and while Kitty bounded out of the window, and ran down the hill with a light, merry laugh, she walked with a slow, guilty step, and calling Kitty, begging her "never to tell."

"No, I shan't think of it again," said Kitty, as she hurried into her father's house, close by the school-room. Ruth could not say the same; she thought of it again and again, and often said to herself, "I don't see why I feel bad. *I didn't steal.* I have done no harm. Charley's books are safe in his desk." The old clock ticked on, and seemed to say, "Ruth, what have you done? what have you done?" "Nothing, replied Ruth over and over again, and just before midnight sank into an uneasy slumber.

Ruth was a thief, although Charley's books were safe in his desk. The Bible says, *"As a man thinketh in his heart, so is he."* She first *coveted* the books, and then even tried to make her friend steal; and nothing but the fear of being found out kept her from taking them from the desk. God saw her heart, and in his eyes, she was a thief. No wonder she tossed and groaned upon her bed, and could find no rest. No rest can be found for her, but in repenting of her sin, and asking God to forgive her, and keep her in the future from wishing for things that do not belong to her. God looks through the outward conduct at the heart, and the boy or girl who partakes of anything which has been stolen, or makes up his mind to deny something he has done, in case he is accused, or tempts his companions to sin, may try to comfort himself by saying, *"I did not steal;"* *"I did not lie;"* *"I've done no harm;"* yet the solemn words, "As a man thinketh in his heart, so is he;" will be spoken in his ears by the voice of a guilty conscience.

~ The Queen and the Child ~

The gardener of a queen of Germany had a little daughter, with whose religious instruction he had taken great pains. When this child was five years of age, the queen saw her one day while visiting the royal garden, and was so much pleased with her that a week afterwards she expressed a wish to see the little girl again. The father brought the child to the palace, and a page conducted her into the royal presence. When she saw the queen, she kissed her robe and modestly took the seat that had been placed for her by the queen's order. From this spot she could overlook the table at which the queen was dining with the ladies of her court; and they watched with interest to see the effect of so much splendor on the simple child. She looked carelessly on the costly dresses of the royal party, the gold dishes on the table, and the pomp with which all was conducted; and then folding her hands, she sang with her clear, childish voice —

> "Jesus! Thy blood and righteousness
> Are all my ornament and dress;
> Fearless, with these pure garments on,
> I'll view the splendors of Thy throne."

All the assembly were struck with surprise at seeing so much feeling and piety in one so young. Tears filed the eyes of the ladies; and the queen exclaimed, "Ah, happy child! how far are we below you!"

~ *Disappointment* ~

"Oh good, good! Oh delightful, delightful! Papa and mama are coming home in the sea-ship Pacific! Oh, how happy, how happy I am!" shouted little Bessie as she jumped up and down, and ran upstairs and downstairs, telling the joyful news to one and another, till everyone in the house was acquainted with it. It seemed as if she could not wait the week that was expected to elapse before the arrival of the Pacific, so anxious was she to greet the dear parents from whom she had been separated a year.

By the next steamer, three days later, came a letter which caused great grief to little

Bessie, and her lamentations were as loud and as long as her expressions of pleasure had been.

"Oh, dear, it is too bad! They could not get berths on the Pacific, and they must wait for the next steamer. Oh, what a disappointment! Everything always happens this way to me; just as I am hoping very much for something, I am sure to be disappointed!" and Bessie covered her face with her hands, and the tears streamed through her little fingers.

"Bessie, my daughter," said her good grandmother, "God orders all things, and all that he does is right."

Bessie murmured something behind the little hands which covered her face, that sounded very like, "Well, I think he might let my papa and mama come in the Pacific, when I want to see them so much."

The steamer in which her parents sailed was wafted pleasantly and safely over the seas, and in due time little Bessie was clasped in the arms of her fond parents, but nothing was heard of the Pacific. "No tidings of the Pacific!" headed one column of the papers for days, then weeks, and then no more was said about it, and people gave up thinking about it — all but those whose homes and hearths are desolate, and to whose hearts the very name of the Pacific will ever send a pang.

When little Bessie heard that the noble steamer was given up as lost, she said, "Mama, I think God was very good not to let you sail in the Pacific."

"Oh, you now think He was good, do you?" answered her mother; "but I heard of a little girl who did not think God was very good, when she first heard that her parents were not coming in that vessel."

"Yes, that was I, mama; but I did not know that the Pacific would be lost."

"And would not God have been as good, if we had sailed in the Pacific and been lost? Listen, Bessie. God has a great plan by which he governs this world of ours. He formed it before this earth was made, and this plan does not change; and we creatures of His are always working out this plan, though we think we do what we choose to do. It was part of his plan that we should not come in the Pacific, and therefore we found it impossible to get berths; and it was also part of His plan that others should sail in her, and, so far as we know, be lost; and though we cannot see the reasons, it is all right.

"Sometimes He disappoints us, and does not let us see the reasons why He does it. Sometimes, as in our case, we see how much better it was for us to be disappointed. One blessed assurance we have, my daughter, is that 'all things work together for good to those who love Him.' Oh, how happy should we be if we could learn in all things to *trust* Him, knowing that all He does is right, whether our blind eyes ever see it or not, or whether or not our wishes are granted!"

Judge not the Lord by feeble sense,
But *trust* Him for His grace;
Behind a frowning providence
He hides a smiling face.

~ *Love's Confidence* ~

There are times when we learn as much from our children as they learn from us. There is something in the artless simplicity of childhood that proves stronger than the care-worn severity of mature years.

I was sitting on the porch at evening, musing too doubtfully upon the future, and letting the clouds of care darken the beauty of a brilliant sunset. I will not say what burdens weighed upon my spirit – but just then, little feet were heard, and my child ran gaily into my extended arms. Catching the playful spirit of my girl, I seized her in my hands and held her over the railings as if to let her fall. Astonished at her lack of fear, I said, "What, not afraid? Why don't you cry? Won't I let you fall?"

"No, *papa, you love me so dearly!*" was her instant reply.

I cannot tell you what instruction flooded through my soul. These words of perfect confidence lingered in my ears. Is it impossible that a father's love should let the child fall, who lies smiling in his arms? How then can the heavenly Father let fall the children who trust in Him? Every doubt is rebuked, and every dark foreboding put to the blush, by the lesson that this child has uttered. Are we not the sons of God? And is our future destiny too sublime for comprehension, so that it doth not yet appear what we shall be; and so shall we fear to be at peace in our Father's arms? If He did not refuse the greatest mercy, but "delivered Him up for us all," will He not also freely give us all things? With any adequate idea of our relations to God as His adopted ones, can we justify one doubt, can we harbor one fear as to the future? If God is our Father, does He not love us too dearly to let any evil befall us? Will He not make all things work together for our good?

~ God Counts ~

A brother and sister were playing in the dining-room, when their mother set a basket of cakes on the tea-table and then stepped outside.

"How nice they look!" said the boy reaching to take one. His sister earnestly objected, and even drew back his hand, repeating that it was against their mother's directions.

"She did not count them," said he.

"But perhaps God did," answered the sister.

So he withdrew from the temptation, and sitting down, seemed to meditate. "You are right," replied he, looking at her with a cheerful, yet serious air, "God *does count*. For the Bible says, that 'the hairs of our head are all numbered.'"

~ The Nettle ~

Jane Stevens came from the garden into the house one morning, crying bitterly. She had not learned to bear pain very heroically, and she had been badly nettled.

"What is the matter, Jane?" said her mother.

"I've got nettled."

"Nettled! how?"

"I was picking currants, and there was a great, ugly nettle in the currant bushes, and so I got stung with it."

"You should have been more careful."

"Well, I didn't see it; besides, it had no business to be there. It was no place for a nettle."

"That is very true," replied her mother, smiling. "It is no place for it, and Tom should have seen that it was removed. But come here, and I will put something on your hand which will make it feel better."

Jane's hand was soon relieved, and she thought no more about the matter that morning.

In the afternoon her cousin Lucy came to see her. "I've come to spend the afternoon; mother has given me leave," said Lucy.

"Oh, I am so glad!" said Jane; and away the two girls skipped to their play.

In an hour, however, Jane came into the house, looking quite out of sorts, and Lucy was not with her.

"Where is Lucy?" asked Jane's mother.

"She has gone home."

"Gone home! What does that mean? I thought she had come to spend the afternoon."

"She didn't want to stay any longer," said Jane, hurrying away from her mother, as if she wished to avoid being asked any more questions.

Her mother saw that something was wrong; but she saw also that Jane did not wish to be questioned; and as Lucy had already gone, she thought she would say no more to her at that time.

Jane went straight to her own room, and there she remained until she was called down to tea. When she came to the tea-table, her mother saw that she had been crying. After tea, she called her to her own room, and said, gently but firmly,

"Now, Jane, you must tell me what happened between you and Lucy this afternoon. I heard her say when she came, that her mother had given her permission to spend the afternoon. It is not often that little girls decline to avail themselves of such a permission. Now I wish you to tell me frankly, just as it is, why your cousin Lucy went home."

"I will tell you, mother," said Jane; "for I have been very unhappy about it ever since. While we were playing in the garden, I asked Lucy to go with me into the meadow, and gather some wild flowers. But she did not wish to go, because she wanted to come into the house and play with my great doll. She said that she had asked her mother to let her come on purpose, to play with it. I was vexed with her, because she would not go into the meadow, and declared that I would not bring out the doll that afternoon. Then she got angry, and said if I were going to be so cross she would not stay with me — she would go home.

'You don't mean to go home, I know,' I said. 'Aunt Lucy said you might stay until night, and I guess you will be glad enough to stay.'

'No, I shan't stay,' she said; 'I shall go home;' and she turned to go out of the garden. I thought she was only trying to frighten me and make me bring out my doll; but the first thing I knew, she was out of the garden and the yard, and running toward home as fast as she could. When I saw that she was really gone, I was sorry for what I had done."

"And what have you been about all the time since Lucy went away?"

"I have been up in my room, crying."

"I should think so, by the look of your eyes. I think you and Lucy both have been pretty badly nettled this afternoon, and I think it is time that the great, ugly nettle was pulled up."

Jane looked at her mother, as if not quite certain what she meant.

"You have not forgotten how you were nettled this morning, have you?"

"No, mother."

"And don't you remember that you said the garden was no place for a nettle?"

"Yes, mother."

"What you said was very true. The garden was no place for it. It should not have been suffered to grow there. Go out, my dear, and see if you can find it there now."

Jane went to the spot where the nettle was growing in the morning, but it was not there, and she went in and told her mother that it was gone.

"So I expected, my dear, for I ordered Thomas today to pull it up. Now the spirit of unkindness in your heart, my child, is like that ugly, stinging nettle. Do you think it should be suffered to grow there? Think of the mischief it has done, and the pain it has caused today. Lucy came here this afternoon, hoping to have a very pleasant visit, and a grand time with your doll, which she has only seen but once, and so it is quite an attraction to her. When she came, you both skipped out into the garden as happy as lambs; but your unkindness spoiled it all. She was your guest, and you know that you should have done all you could to make her visit pleasant. But instead of doing this you were disobliging, and positively unkind, and your unkindness sent her home feeling very unhappy. Don't you think it worse to have the heart stung than the hands? And this same ugly nettle has stung you as well as Lucy. Is it not so? Had you not rather bear the pain of being nettled this morning, than the self-reproach which you have felt for treating her as you did?"

"Yes, mother, I am sure I had; for I have been very unhappy this afternoon."

"The nettle in the garden has been pulled up and thrown away. What shall be done with that ugly weed of unkindness and selfishness that has sprung up in your heart? Would it not be a fine plan if that could be pulled up, too? So long as it remains, it will be stinging someone, as it did this afternoon. Who do you suppose planted the nettle in the garden?

"Planted the nettle, mother! I never heard of such a thing as planting a nettle. They come up of themselves quite fast enough."

"Did you ever hear of corn and potatoes coming up of themselves?"

"No, mother; I guess Thomas would like it if they would."

"So it was with our hearts, my daughter. *They* may be compared to a garden. The weeds of unkindness, selfishness, and pride come up by themselves. They need no cultivation. If we take no care of our hearts, these will be sure to grow vicious enough. But the beautiful plants of love, gentleness, kindness, and self-denial will not grow without culture. Again, let me ask you, what shall be done with the seed of unkindness in your heart? Shall it be permitted to grow there, or will you try to pull it up?"

Jane looked at her mother, and replied, earnestly and seriously, "I will try to get rid of it, mother. I know it has done a great deal of mischief already. I don't want it to grow in my heart any longer."

"I am glad to hear you say so; but you must remember that one effort will not suffice. Do you suppose that Thomas will never have to pull up another nettle in the garden?"

"I know he will have to pull up many nettles. I know they keep growing all the time."

"Let this teach you a lesson, my dear. You must watch your heart all the time, if you will keep down the weeds. When unkind thoughts arise, you must try to overcome them, while you carefully cultivate every kind and gentle emotion. If you do this faithfully, the nettles of your heart will not grow rank enough to sting your friends, as they did this afternoon. But the beautiful plants, which you carefully cultivate, will rejoice the hearts of all who love you. You must, however, remember that it is only by constant watchfulness that you can subdue the ever-springing weeds of evil in your heart. You must watch, that you may be able to uproot them as soon as they appear, before they obtain a firmer hold; and you must pray, because you need help to do this. It is too great a work for you to do in your own strength; but there is One who will help you, if you will ask Him."

~ *The Mountain Storm* ~

Janet Ray lived with her mother in a lonely cottage on the mountain-side. It was far away from the rest of the world, but they had not always lived alone there. Mrs. Ray's two sons went away from their mother to go to sea, and Mrs. Ray intended to leave her solitary cottage, and before winter find a home among the little cottages at the foot of the mountain. But she was so much attached to her own picturesque home where she had lived many years, that she delayed leaving it as long as possible. All through the lingering autumn there was more freedom for Janet, who was enterprising, and fond of mounting some of the greatest heights in search of flowers. She would go, too, every day down to the glen, where their friends lived, who would fill her basket with some delicacy to take to her mother, and every day asked when she was coming down to live among them.

One day, as Janet left her mother's house for one of these daily visits, both she and her mother saw how threateningly the clouds were gathering.

"I fear there is going to be a storm," said Mrs. Ray. "I am almost afraid to let you go down through the glen. If it should surprise you, and delay you in coming home, it would give me great anxiety."

"Oh, do not be afraid," said Janet. "If there is going to be a storm, there is more need we should have something to eat in the house, and I shall be back before you have time to be anxious."

Janet set forth, but among the mountains it began to snow before she had been long gone. She, meanwhile, had passed through the glen, and had reached the little huts in the valley.

"I'm surprised to see you," said her mother's friend, Anne Ross, "or rather, I wish your mother had come with you. Donald was saying this morning, your mother ought to be safely housed among us. And today it looks quite threatening."

Janet promised that she would urge her mother to move directly, nor did she linger long, but exchanged some of her own and her mother's crafts for the supplies they would need, and then set out homeward.

Her path led up the glen, and she could not help stopping to admire how the swollen stream dashed over the rocks. Presently the rushing current impeded her way, and she soon met the storm of snow that was fast increasing. She hurried on through the blinding flakes, and by the rising stream, and then she had to leave the water-course and climb up the hill-side. She found the snow had been fast increasing for some hours, and it was difficult to keep her footing in the midst of the deepening drifts. She kept courageously on, till at last her strength failed her.

"My mother, how frightened she will be for me!" she thought, "and am I quite without help?"

Then she remembered how in stormy nights, when she and her mother had fancied her two brothers were struggling against storms upon the sea, her mother had always ended in saying, "God is there as well as here. They are in his hands, and I could not ask a better protection, even were they close by my side."

"And so she is praying for me now," said Janet to herself. "God is here as well as there, and his arms will uphold me, even in death," she added, for the snow was folding about her chillingly.

Then she began to sing with a loud voice,
"The Lord is my refuge!,"
for she was beginning to feel benumbed with the cold. And she thought if her mother should come out to find her, she would send out her voice to meet her.

Meantime, Donald Ross had returned home, and when he found that Janet had been down into the glen, and had set out to return, he was very much alarmed.

"You should not have let her go back," he said to his wife. "The snow is gathering fast among the mountains and I do not know how Janet can get home alive."

He set out directly with his dog, and one or two of his neighbors, in the steps of Janet. With difficulty they made their way up the glen, the drifting snow clouded still more in the dying light, and they could not decide at what point

Janet would have left the glen. The men took different paths, and Donald followed one path, which his dog, who seemed to understand the purpose of their search, eagerly led him on. Yet even the dog seemed uncertain, for Janet had lost her usual course, and had been wandering blindly through the snow.

At length, Donald himself reached the cottage, and found that Janet had not been there. The poor mother was frantic, and had been calling Janet's name in every direction, and had herself searched in vain among the drifts. Donald went back upon the search again, with his dog, and just as the faithful animal had started forward, as if he had come upon the scent, Donald heard a voice in the distance. He hastened on, and found Janet sinking in the snow, her breath almost gone, but still singing out the words of the hymn. She was hardly conscious when Donald took her in his arms. He carried her to the cottage, and by the warmth from the fire, she opened her eyes, and said:

"Ah, mother, God was there as well as here. I had no fear in His arms, and I trusted that you, too, felt him near."

~ Minnie's Pet ~

Once, when I was in England, I visited some friends, who lived in a pleasant part of the country. They had a fine old house, filled with all sorts of beautiful things; but nothing indoors was so delightful as the wide, green lawn with its smooth, soft turf, and the garden, with its laburnums and lilies, and violets, and hosts upon hosts of roses. There was a pretty silvery fountain playing among the flowers, so close to a little bower of honeysuckles, that the butterflies fluttering about them had to be very careful, or before they knew it, they would have their wings soaked through and through with the spray.

About the house and grounds were all kinds of beautiful pets: greyhounds and spaniels, and lap-dogs, and rare white kittens, gay parrots, and silver pheasants, and sweet-singing canaries; but here in this pleasant spot, right under the honeysuckle bower, all alone by himself, in a large green cage, sat an ugly gray owl. He was the crossest, surliest old fellow I ever saw in all my life. I tried very hard to make friends with him; but it was of no use; he never treated me with decent civility. And one day, when I was offering him a bit of cake, he caught my finger and bit it till it bled; and I said to Mrs. M—, "What *do* you keep that cross old creature for?"

I noticed that my friend looked sad, when she answered me and said, "We only keep him for our dear little Minnie's sake; he was her pet."

Now I had never heard of her little Minnie; so I asked about her, and was told this story:

Minnie was a sweet, gentle little girl, who loved everybody, and every creature that God had made; and everybody and every creature she met loved her. Rough people were gentle to her, and cross people became kindly around her; she could go straight up to vicious horses, and fierce dogs, and spiteful cats, and they would become quiet and mild. I don't think anything could resist her loving ways, unless it were a mad bull or a setting hen.

One night as Minnie lay awake in her little bed, in the nursery, listening to a summer rain, she heard a strange fluttering and scratching in the chimney, and she called her nurse and said, "Biddy! What is that funny noise up there?"

Biddy listened a moment and said, "Surely it's nothing but a stray rook. Now he's quite gone away; so go to sleep wid ye, my darling."

Minnie tried to go to sleep, like a good girl; but after awhile she heard that sound again, and presently something came fluttering and scratching right down into the grate, and out into the room! Minnie called again to Biddy, but Biddy was tired and sleepy, and *wouldn't* wake up. It was so dark that Minnie could see nothing, and she felt a little strange; but she was no coward, and as the bird seemed very quiet, she went to sleep again after awhile, and dreamed that great flocks of rooks were flying over slowly, and darkening the sky with their jet-black wings.

She woke very early in the morning, and the first thing she saw was a great gray owl, perched on the bed-post at her feet, staring at her with his big, round eyes. He did not fly off when she started up in bed, but only ruffled up his feathers, and said, "Who!" Minnie had never seen an owl before; but she was not afraid, and she answered merrily, "You'd better say 'Who!' Why, who are you yourself, you queer old wonder-eyes?"

Then she woke Biddy, who was dreadfully frightened, and called up the butler, who caught the owl and put him into a cage.

This strange bird was always rather ill-natured and gruff to everybody but Minnie; he seemed to take kindly to her from the first. So he was called "Minnie's pet," and nobody disputed her right to him. He would take food from her little hands and never peck her; he would perch on her shoulder, and let her take him on an airing round the garden; and sometimes, he would sit and watch her studying her lesson, and look as wise and solemn as a learned professor, till he would fall to winking and blinking and go off into a sound sleep.

Minnie grew really fond of this pet, grave and unsocial as he was; but she always called him by the funny name she had given him first — *"Old Wonder-eyes."*

In the winter-time little Minnie was taken ill, and she grew worse and worse, till her friends all knew that she was going to leave them very soon. Darling little Minnie was not sorry to die. As she had loved everybody and every creature that God had made, and loved God too, she was not afraid to go to Him when He called her.

The day before she died, she gave all her pets to her brothers and sisters, but she said to her mother, "*You* take good care of poor old Wonder-eyes, for he'll have nobody to love him when I am gone."

The owl missed Minnie very much. Whenever he heard anyone coming he would cry, "Who!" and when he found it wasn't his friend, he would ruffle up his feathers, and look as though he felt himself insulted. He grew crosser and crosser every day, till there would have been no bearing with him, if it had not been for the memory of Minnie.

The next time I saw the old owl, sitting glaring and growling on his perch, I understood why he was so unhappy and sullen. My heart ached for him — but so did the finger he had bitten; and I did not venture very near, to tell him how sorry I was for him. When I think of him now, I don't blame him, but pity him for his crossness: and I always say to myself, "*Poor old Wonder-eyes!*" Little reader, if you are kind to birds and animals, they will be kind to you; but if you are cross to them, they will be cross to you.

~ *Procrastination* ~

Does any bright-eyed little boy or girl wonder what that long word means? It means delaying, putting off to another time what ought to be done just now.

Ellen has some work to do before she goes to school. She can easily get it done, long before school-time, if she begins it when she can. But it is very pleasant out in the garden, where Ellen is playing with her little brother James; and as often as her conscience whispers to her, "You ought to go in and do that work now, Ellen," the little girl answers, "Oh! there's time enough yet. I can hurry and get it done in a few minutes," and Ellen goes on with her play.

By and by a whisper comes a little louder than before: "It is eight o'clock, Ellen; you ought to go in."

"Well, I will go," Ellen thinks in reply. "I will go in very soon. There's plenty of time yet, though."

"Ellen!" called the little girl's mother, from the window, "come in, my child, and finish that work, before the bell rings for school."

"Yes, mother, just as soon as I've had one more race with James," and Ellen runs laughing around the garden, in pursuit of her little brother.

"Half-past eight," she exclaims, as hot and out of breath, she hurries at last into the house. "I had no idea it was so late."

Tired and in a hurry, Ellen sits down to her work. She can sew both well and rapidly, but fifteen minutes is a very short space of time for all that she has to do. And then her hands tremble, and her cotton seems to take a strange pleasure in getting into knots, and her needle breaks, and altogether it is almost nine o'clock when her work is done.

"You will be late at school," her mother says, as Ellen folds her work and lays it hastily aside. "You should not have played so long, my child."

There is the trouble with these people who are continually putting things off. They always think they have time enough. They wait till the very last minute before they begin their work, then they begin it all in a hurry, and leave it only half done.

A much better way is to begin everything at the right time, and leave it at the right time, *done, and well done.*

~ *Little Kindnesses* ~

"'Tis sweet to do something
for those that we love
Though the favour be ever so small."

Brothers, sisters, did you ever see the good effect which little acts of kindness produce, within that charming circle that we call home? We love to receive little favours ourselves; and how pleasant the reception of them makes the circle! To draw up the arm chair and get the slippers for father, to watch if any little service can be rendered for mother, to assist brother or help sister, how pleasant it makes home!

A little boy has a hard lesson given him at school, and his teacher asks him if he thinks he can get it; for a moment the little fellow hangs down his head, but the next moment he looks brightly up to say, "I can get my sister to help me!" That is right, sister, help little brother, and you are binding a tie round his heart that may save him in many an hour of dark temptation.

"I don't know how to do this sum, but brother will show me," says another little one.

"Sister, I've dropped a stitch in my knitting; I tried to pick it up, but it has run down, and I can't fix it."

The little girl's face is flushed, and she watches her sister with a nervous anxiety while she replaces the "naughty stitch."

"Oh, I am so glad!" she says, as she receives it again from the hands of her sister all nicely arranged; "you are a good girl, Mary."

"Bring it to me sooner next time, and then it won't get so bad!" says the gentle voice of Mary. The little one bounds away with a light heart to finish her task.

If Mary had not helped her, she would have lost her walk in the garden. Surely it is better to do as Mary did, than to say, "Oh, go away, and don't trouble me;" or to scold the little one all the time you are performing the trifling favour.

Little acts of kindness, gentle words, loving smiles, they strew the path of life with flowers; they make the sun shine brighter and the green earth greener; and He who taught us "love one another," looks with favour upon the gentle and kind-hearted, and He pronounces the meek blessed.

Brothers, sisters, love one another, bear with one another. If one offends, forgive and love him still; and whatever may be the faults of others, we must remember that, in the sight of God, we have others as great and perhaps greater than theirs.

Be kind to the little ones; they will often be fretful and wayward. Be patient with them, and amuse them. How often a whole family of little ones is restored to good humour by an elderly member proposing some new play, and perhaps joining in it, or gathering them around her while she relates some pleasant story!

And brothers, do not think, because you are stronger, that it is unmanly to be gentle to your little brothers and sisters. True nobleness of heart and true manliness of conduct are never coupled with pride and arrogance.

Nobility and gentleness go hand in hand; and when I see a young gentleman kind and respectful to his mother and gentle and forbearing to his brothers and sisters, I think he has a noble heart.

Ah! Many a mother and sister's heart has been pained to tears by the cold neglect and stiff unkindness of those young men whom God has made their natural protectors.

Brothers, sisters, never be unkind to one another, never be ashamed to help one another, never be ashamed to help anyone, and you will find that though it is pleasant to receive favours, it is more blessed to give than to receive.

~ The Two Holidays ~

"I do so count on tomorrow," said Agnes to a young friend whom she happened to meet. "Mama is going to take me into the country for a day's pleasure, and we are to call for my aunt, and cousins Charlotte and Henry, to go with us. And mama says we may ramble about in the fields wherever we like, if we do not go too far out of sight. We can go into the hay-fields and help make hay, and perhaps I shall be covered up in some, and mama and aunt will try to find me. And Henry intends to take the new fishing tackle, which his papa gave him, and perhaps he will let Charlotte and me try to fish. Oh, it will be so delightful! I intend to be up at six o'clock, ready to start as soon as mama is willing."

Perhaps, if Agnes had been a little more thoughtful, she would not have said quite so much about a pleasure in which her friend could not join her. The little friend had been ill, and though now recovering, was fatigued with having walked for only a quarter of an hour. Agnes did not mean to be unkind, for she was an affectionate child; but so it is sometimes, even with older persons than Agnes, the present enjoyment, or the anticipation of any great pleasure, occupies their attention so entirely, that they become unmindful of the feelings of others. A lady once related all the particulars of a birthday gathering of her eldest daughter, to a friend who had buried her only child but three months before. She would have been very sorry if she had known the pain she gave.

Agnes went to bed early that night, full of bright visions of the coming day, but when she opened her eyes in the morning, a steady rain threatened to disappoint all her hopes. When she came down to breakfast, she looked first at her mama, then at the rain, and then at her mama again. At last she said, "How very unfortunate this rain is!" and added, rather doubtfully, "but I suppose, mama, you intend to go; I daresay it will be fine by the time we get there."

Her mama shook her head, and replied, "It is *just possible* that the rain may cease in an hour or two, but I think it more *likely* that it will continue the greater part of the day; at any rate, I should not choose to risk it. You know I made the engagement conditionally, with your aunt, and I am sure *she* will not expect us, whatever Charlotte and Henry may do. So you must content yourself at home today, and we will go the first fine morning that is convenient. However, to make you some amends for the disappointment, I give you leave to spend your time as you like."

Agnes was grievously disappointed, and did not think it possible that anything could make her happy that day; but as she was on the whole a good girl, and moreover had a high opinion of her mama's judgment, she did not look cross, or discontented, but was willing to give up going. And, indeed, after the first feeling was over, the idea of spending a day at home just as she liked, rather took her fancy.

But she soon found, as many others have done, that liberty to do as we like, is not sufficient to make us happy. It is *the way in which we spend our time* that makes us happy or otherwise.

It was a long time before Agnes could make up her mind what exactly to do; she took up a book and read a little, but it did not interest her, because her mind was too unsettled to attend to it. She spent a few minutes at some fancy work, of which she was generally fond, and then opened a portfolio to look at the pictures, but nothing would do — the rain, the rain, as it continued to descend — she could not help gazing at that.

At last she went upstairs to her own room, and from a drawer that contained her treasures, took out, one by one, the little presents that had been made to her at different times by kind friends and companions, a goodly collection of books and trinkets, and I know not how many things beside. These engaged her attention, but they did not make her cheerful. She had just put them all away when the dinner bell rang, and very glad she was to go down to her mama, who had taken advantage of the wet morning to attend to some little matters which otherwise had been deferred.

While they were sitting for a dinner, the clouds began to part, the rain ceased for a while, and it became clear, in the midst of which the sun broke forth in such glory that it caused a rainbow, that Agnes thought exceeded in beauty all the rainbows she had ever seen. Whether it was really so, or whether it was only her feelings at the time that made her *think* so, we will not say; perhaps she could not decide the point herself.

"Agnes," said her mama, who noticed her little girl's sad countenance when she came down, "what are you going to do this afternoon?"

"Indeed, mama, I do not know. I don't get on very well by myself."

"Well, then, since we have been disappointed of our intended holiday, we will go, now that it is fine, and try to put a little holiday feeling into the hearts of our neighbours, and so make a holiday, though of a different kind from that which we had anticipated."

"Oh, yes, mama, I should like that very much; where shall we go?"

"We will call on old Susan, and take the half-crown Mrs. Smith was so kind to give me yesterday. Then we can leave the book for William Brown. And I have been told this morning of a poor old woman who has lately lost her husband, and has six little children, for whom she can scarcely get food or clothing. I have put up some left-over clothes, which Mary can go with us to carry, and I intend to give them as much money as I should have spent for my holiday, if I had gone. But I will not disappoint you of *your* holiday. I will let you have the money it will cost, and you can go some day with your aunt and cousins."

"What, and leave you at home, mama? Oh, I could not bear to go so. Besides, if you give up your holiday, I will give up mine, if you will let them have that money too."

"Most willingly, my dear; but I wish you to do just as you like, so consider well before you decide."

"My mind is made up, mama."

"Well then, we will go together; here is your money, for it *is* yours now that you have relinquished the holiday, and *you* shall have the pleasure of giving it, while *I* shall rejoice to think my own dear little girl has begun to exercise that self-denial which I hope she will continue to manifest as long as she lives."

I will not tell of the many thanks Agnes and her mama received, nor of the tears of joy which they witnessed; but when Agnes told me this story of her youthful days, in her old age, she assured me it was the happiest holiday she had ever enjoyed.

~ Cobwebs ~

"Oh! Oh, mother, mother! Oh! Oh! Oh!" cried little Ellie, as she burst into the room where her mother was sitting.

"What *is* the matter, my child?" asked her mother.

"Nothing, mother," said Herbert, who had followed Ellie; "only there's a spider on her dress, and I *told* her it wouldn't hurt her."

Now Herbert was very fond of butterflies, and bugs, and all kinds of insects. He did not kill them, because he knew it would be wrong to kill the little creatures God had made, just to please himself. But when he found a dead one, that had pretty eyes, or feet, or wings, he brought them into the house, and asked his mother to fasten it upon a sheet of pasteboard, so that he could keep it, and to tell him all she knew about it. Of course he was not afraid of a spider; and he thought Ellie was very foolish to be frightened so much.

But poor little Ellie, whose dress was torn, and whose hair was flying in every direction, was sobbing so that she could scarcely speak. By the time, however, that her mother had turned her around four or five times without finding any spider, she had quieted; and when her mother asked again, "What was the matter, my child?" she said,

"Why, mother, I saw some *beads* up in the bushes — prettier than mine — yes, as bright as the looking-glass; and I wanted them to put around the baby's neck, and I almost had got them in my hand, and a great spider — Oh! mother, mother!" and the tears came again, and Ellie couldn't finish her story. The mother thought she had known older people than Ellie try very hard to get something because it glittered, and find after all it was only a cobweb. But she knew Ellie wouldn't understand if she told her this, so she didn't say it.

"Well," says some little boy, who, being as Herbert was, about two years older than Ellie, thinks himself a great deal wise, "she *was* foolish if she thought cobwebs looked like beads. *I* don't think they look like beads *at all*." Don't you, sir? What time did you get up this morning? You "don't know?" Well, which got up first, you or the sun? Ah! I see. You have lived six, seven, or eight summers, and have always let the sun get up before you. Now, sir, just to please *me*, do you, tomorrow or the first bright summer morning, get up just a little before the sun. Be quick, for the sun doesn't have any dressing to do, and his eyes are bright without his staying to wash them. So if you don't take care, he will be up, and looking round among the trees and bushes before you. As soon as you are washed, and dressed, and brushed, go out among the trees. Oh! you "live in the *city*," and there are no trees there, and you "can't go see the sun to know when he *is* coming up." What a pity! Then you are not at all to blame for not knowing that cobwebs sometimes look like beads. Ellie lived in the country. But she was a very little girl, and didn't know much more about it than you do.

So she said, "Mother, who hung these bright beads up in the tree?"

"Ellie, said her mother, "don't you know that when you go outside in the morning the grass is all wet, and there are drops of water on all the bushes? It is what we call *dew*. It comes in the night; not like the rain, but very gently and silently; and all the little flowers, that looked so sad and weary, when the hot sun shone on them, hold up their cups and drink them full of the cool, fresh dew. So in the morning they seem all bright and happy again. The spiders, Ellie, weave their webs in the trees, and weave them of such tiny threads, that when they are dry, you can scarcely see them. But when the dew comes out, it gathers in round balls, or beads, all over the web, and when the morning sun shines on the beads, they sparkle like diamonds, so bright that if they *were* diamonds, Victoria or Eugenie would wish them as my little Ellie did."

Just then from under Ellie's pink apron came a large brown spider. There it had lain hidden all this time, and had not hurt her at all. So you see she need not have been so much afraid of it. Ellie didn't move, but she drew a very long breath, and her blue eyes were wide open, while she watched her mother brush him off upon the floor. They opened wider still when instead of a spider, there lay upon the floor a small brown ball, and near it, creeping in all directions, were ever so many little spiders, not as large as the head of a pin. Ellie stepped first one way, and then the other, but being afraid to run either way among so many dangers, she climbed into her mother's lap.

"Are spiders made as quick as that?" asked Herbert.

Their mother laughed, and told them that when some kinds of spiders wished to carry their little ones anywhere, they take them on their backs; and that she supposed when these little spiders saw such a great animal as Ellie was, so near their home, they were frightened, and ran and clambered upon their mother; and their mother was so frightened she didn't know which way to go, and jumped upon Ellie's dress. To which mother asked, "Which, then

Ellie, do you suppose was the most frightened – the little spiders, or the large spider, or Ellie?" Ellie thought *she* was.

"Oh! look, look!" said Herbert, and sure enough the little brown ball was unrolling itself and becoming a spider again, all ready to run away.

Then Mrs. Elliot, for that was the name of the children's mother, told Herbert and Ellie that some spiders, when they think a person is going to hurt them, roll themselves up very quickly into a ball, and drop upon the earth, where they look so much like a little ball of dirt, that they escape danger.

"Why, mother," said Herbert, "I did not think spiders knew enough for that."

"How do the spiders make their little webs?" asked Ellie.

"I'll tell you a story," said Mrs. Elliot. "One day your Auntie Lizzie was lying on a lounge which stood close by a window, and a large spider came to the outside of the window. First he spun a little thread from the lower corner of one side of the window to the upper corner on the other side. Then he went to the upper corner on the other side and spun another thread to the other lower corner. So he spun a good many threads, fastening them along the sides of the sash, and making them cross each other in the center, till his web looked like the spokes of a wheel. Then he went almost to the center of it and jumped from spoke to spoke, spinning a little thread and fastening it to each spoke as he crossed it, till he had fastened a thread quite around the center, and about half the length of your finger from it. Then he went a little further off and spun another ring, and so on, until his web almost covered the lower window sash. This took him about two hours. Just as he had it nicely finished, there came a gust of wind, which whirled the sticks and straw and dead leaves all about in the air. When it was over, the spider's web was full of dirt, and looked as if it was quite spoiled. Well, what did the spider do? Do you suppose he got angry, as some children would have done, and stamped, and said, 'I'll never spin another web as long as I live?' Not a bit of it. He went very patiently to work picking out bits of straw and dead leaves and dust. But after a while he seemed to get discouraged, for he stopped, went to the center of the web, and stood for some time looking all about him. Then he started again and went very rapidly along one of the spokes, cutting off from it all the little threads that ran around the web. Then he went to the next spoke and cut off the threads where he had fastened them there. Where the threads were soiled or broken he threw them away. Those that were good he rolled in balls, and, like the economical little fellow he was, placed them together in the center of his web. By the time he had gone in this way all over his web, it was too dark to watch him any longer. But at daylight the next morning his web was nicely finished and hung, covered with dewdrops, sparkling in the morning sun. Don't you think *that* spider knew something?" asked Mrs. Elliot.

"Yes indeed, mother, said Herbert. "Spiders know almost as much as people, don't they?"

"Oh no, my son," said his mother. "The spider has no soul. It lives a little while and then dies, and that is the last of it. So it only needs to know how to take care of itself and to get its food while it lives here. And so much God has taught it; but that is all. When the spider is first made, it knows just so much, and it never knows any more. A little child when it is first made, scarcely knows as much as a spider. But a child has a soul; a mind which can learn, and keep learning, as long as it lives; which can find out about God, and what God would have it do, so that when it dies it may go to heaven and live with him."

"Mother," asked Ellie, "what do the spiders make webs for?"

"I should think you might know that without asking," said Herbert; "to catch flies, of course."

"But, Herbert," said Mrs. Elliot, "when the flies find themselves in a spider's web, why don't they fly out again?"

Master Herbert's wisdom failed him on this point; but Ellie said, "Perhaps the web sticks to their feet." This was only a "guess" of Ellie's, but she happened to guess right. The threads stick to the fly, and before he can get away, the spider, who has been watching in some sly corner, runs up, spins threads all around him so that he cannot move, and then kills him. The children did not like the spider quite as well when they learned that it is so cruel to little flies. The mother told them that that was the only way the spider had to get its food, and that when flies and other insects were so numerous as to be troublesome, the spider did good by killing them. Still they couldn't quite forgive him. So Mrs. Elliot said, "I will tell you a pleasanter thing about the spider's web. When the spider is on the top of a tree and wishes to go to another tree that is a good way off, he waits until the wind blows directly toward the tree to which he wishes to go. Then he spins a long thread and the wind takes it up and blows it along till it reaches and catches on the right tree. Then Mr. Spider fastens the thread to the tree on which he is standing, and travels to the other tree on a bridge of his own building."

The children laughed heartily at this. Then their mother found for them the song of "The Spider and the Fly." And when they had read it, they ran off to see if they could find any of Mr. Spider's bridges.

~ The Basket of Peaches ~

Half a century ago, that excellent man, the Rev. William Woodbridge, established in the city of Newark a boarding school for young ladies. His residence was on the upper green, in a large stone building, and attached to the house was a large, deep garden, quite filled with fruit trees.

The venerable teacher could sit in his back parlor, and while unobserved, could have a tolerably good view of the entire garden, and of all the young ladies who delighted to frequent it. He was greatly pleased to see his young and joyous flock of charming girls gamboling under the trees, and enjoying the beauties of nature, when robed in the glories of early summer, and he did not fail to improve every opportunity to enforce some valuable truth.

It was about midsummer that he noticed one luxuriant peach tree laden with green fruit, so plentifully that the boughs were bowed down under its weight. He naturally supposed that the beautiful tinge upon the ripening peach might tempt his young friends to taste of the fruit before it was fully ripe; and one lovely afternoon, just before sunset, he called the young ladies into the parlor and most kindly and affectionately explained to them the danger of eating unripe fruit, and urged them to allow it to remain on the tree until perfectly ripe, and he promised that those who refrained from plucking the green fruit, should have it all when matured. Each bright and happy face yielded a full assent to this reasonable proposition, and they ran down into the garden with complete delight.

This tree in particular was an object of great attraction, and the warm days of summer were fast preparing for this happy throng a delicious feast. They daily watched its progress toward maturity, and manifested sometimes no little impatience.

The venerable minister and teacher, as he sat in his back parlor, and as the peaches were fast approaching maturity, could sometimes see the uplifted hand of some young lady plucking the forbidden fruit. He, however, said nothing, until the time arrived when the peaches were perfectly ripe. He had the fruit carefully gathered, and the very choicest of it filled a large basket.

He placed it in the back parlor and called in all the young ladies, and took occasion, on exhibiting it, to enforce his rule, assuring the girls of the joy it now gave him to present them this basket of delicious fruit fully ripe. He then welcomed all who had not plucked any green peaches from the tree to come forward and partake bountifully of the large supply.

To his surprise, all remained motionless except one little girl. She, with a gentle step, approached the venerable teacher. "My dear," said he, "have you not eaten a single peach?"

She laid her little hand upon her breast, and sweetly replied, *"Not one, sir."*

"Then," said the excellent man, "the whole basket-full is yours."

The happy girl took them and distributed them among all her school-fellows. How pure the joy which flowed from obedience, and how pure its reward!

~ Little Rose Clark ~

I am going to tell you a true story about a poor family who lived in the large city of Philadelphia. There is a small court or alley that is in the southern part of the city, and where a great many poor, wicked, forlorn creatures live; and there are many very little children among them. The street is called Belford Street. There is a society which visits this street and does all it can to relieve their wants.

One cold afternoon, last winter, when the snow was falling thick and fast, and the wind was blowing, and everybody was hurrying through the streets to get home to their pleasant fires and their nice warm supper, a poor ragged little girl, without shoes or stockings, stood crying beside a little boy, whom she was trying to keep warm with her own shawl, which she had taken off and thrown around him. Few noticed them, or if they did, they only passed them by, and did not speak to them, only to tell them to go home. Poor children! theirs was a miserable home. And thus they stood, till, in a little while, a gentleman, out of curiosity, stopped and asked them where they lived and why the little girl had no shoes or stockings.

"We live in Belford street, sir, and my father is a weaver; mother winds spools; but now father is sick, and cannot do any work, and mother can only earn *eight cents* a day. Willie and I have to go out a-begging; we've been out all day, and this is all we've got." So saying, she opened her apron, where she had a few hard stale crusts, and a bone with a little meat on it.

The gentleman gave them money to buy some good bread with, and promised to come and see them, as soon as he could go home. He then went to a shop and purchased some sugar, and tea, which he took home, and put into a large basket, with some bread and meat, and a few little articles which his wife thought would tempt the poor man's appetite. Calling to his waiter-man John to come and carry the basket, he set off in the storm to find the home of little Rose Clark, which was the beggar child's name, and her brother Willie. The place was soon found – and imagine the gentleman's surprise, when he had to go down a pair of rickety wooden steps into a damp, dark cellar, where, in one corner, was a bed made on the floor, and a poor man in the last stage of consumption! At the foot of the bed was a woman, who had once been pretty, holding in her arms a little babe, a few months old. Near her, fast asleep upon the earthen floor, was the little Willie of whom you have already heard.

"And where is Rose?" asked the gentleman.

"She has gone out to try to get something to make a fire," replied her mother.

Soon after she came in, and when she saw the gentleman, she ran up to him and exclaimed, "I am so glad you have come; see what I have got, two buns for baby, mother and Willie, and a nice orange for father."

"And what have you got for yourself?"

"Nothing; I am not so *very* hungry; I can eat these crusts; I only wish we had some fire, it is so cold."

The gentleman, who was much moved by the generosity of the girl, called her to him, and gave her the basket, telling her to distribute the contents as she pleased. Then calling to John, he bade him make a fire with what he could get, and sent him to a little store for some wood, and soon there was a warm fire burning upon the hearth, and the cellar began to feel less damp.

Mr. B. sat down and talked to the sick man and his wife, and from them he learned their history.

He was a Scotsman, and had come to this country after the birth of his second child; he had plenty of work to do, and a nice home, and a kind and industrious wife, but soon he fell sick and could not do any work. Then his poor wife did what she could, but she too fell sick, and God sent them a dear little one to nurse and take care of. One by one their little stock of furniture went to pay for food, to keep them from starving, till at last, they were forced to live in the cellar where Mr. B. found them.

Shortly after this, Mr. B. left them, promising to come in the morning and bring a physician to see them, and also promising to send John with some good, warm blankets and some clothing for the children. John fixed the fire, and brought some more wood to last over the night, and then bidding Rose good night, he left them.

How much have you, little reader, to thank God for! When you look around upon the thousand blessings you daily enjoy in your comfortable homes, let your heart go up in gratitude to God, remembering that He is the Giver of every good gift. And let your hearts go out in pity to the suffering poor, and in earnest effort to relieve their wants. Every little girl may do something toward relieving human suffering.

~ Telling Mother ~

A cluster of young girls stood about the door of the school-room one afternoon, engaged in close conversation, when a little girl joined them and asked what they were doing. "I am telling the girls a *secret*, Kate, and we will let you know, if you will promise not to tell anyone as long as you live," was the reply.

"I won't tell anyone but my mother," replied Kate; "I tell her everything, for she is my best friend."

"No, not even your mother; no one in the world."

"Well then, I can't hear it; for *what I can't tell my mother is not fit for me to know.*" After speaking this, Kate walked away slowly and perhaps sadly, yet with a quiet conscience, while her companions went on with their secret conversation.

I am sure that if Kate continued to act on that principle, she became a virtuous, useful woman. No child of a pious mother will be likely to take a sinful course, if Kate's reply is taken for a rule of conduct.

As soon as a boy listens to a conversation at school, or on the playground, which he would fear or blush to repeat to his mother, he is in the way of temptation, and no one can tell where he will stop. Many a man dying in disgrace, in prison or on the scaffold, has looked back with bitter remorse to the time when first a sinful companion gained his ear, and came between him and a pious mother. Boys and girls, if you would lead a Christian life, and die a Christian death, make Kate's reply your rule: "What I cannot tell my mother is not fit for me to know;" for a pious mother is your best friend.

If you have no mother, do as the disciples did; go and tell Jesus. He loves you better than the most tender parent.

~ How to Take Medicine ~

Little Amy was sick. She tried all day not to be sick, because she did not like to take medicine. But by four o'clock, she laid her head on her mother's lap and said, "I'm sick, mother." Her mother bathed her head, warmed her feet, and put on her a little new nightgown. Then she placed her in Sarah's arms, while she went downstairs.

"Has she gone to get some medicine, do you think, Sarah?" asked Amy.

"Oh, yes," said Sarah, "nice, good doctor's stuff, not bad at all to take, Amy."

Amy laid her head on Sarah's shoulder, wishing what Sarah said was true. Presently her mother came back, with a wine-glass in her hand.

"Is it bitter, very?" asked the little girl.

"No," cried Sarah; "it is sweet — it is good."

"Mother, is it bitter, and bad to take?" asked Amy.

"Yes, my child, it is bitter, but not bad to take if you make up your mind to take it, like a good child."

Amy had rather know the truth than be deceived. All children do.

"Sarah, it is wicked to call bitter sweet," said she.

Her mother took her in her arms, and held the glass. She did not coax or threaten, or promise her pretty things; she wanted her little child to be willing to take it for the sake of getting well.

"Wait a minute," said Amy, and clasping her little hands together, she shut her eyes and said, "O my Saviour, will you help a poor little child to take her medicine, and be well? Will you please give Amy a mind to do it? Amen."

Amy opened her soft blue eyes, and stretching out her hand, took the glass and swallowed the medicine. Sarah gave her water to rinse her mouth, when she sweetly smiled, saying, "How much little girls can do if they try! And mother, hasn't the Lord Jesus promised to help them?" The mother kissed her darling.

~ *The Hindu Girl* ~

A little Hindu girl, one summer's afternoon, was innocently playing outside her father's cottage, when suddenly she was seized and carried off, taken to Calcutta, and sold as a slave. She was a sweet and beautiful little girl, and the lady who bought her soon began to love her very much, and she thought she should not make her a slave. She had no children of her own, and she liked to have a little girl to play with her and amuse her. She loved her more and more, and, as she grew older, she became her true companion.

When the little girl was stolen from her father, she was too young to have learned his religion. The lady who bought her was a Mahometan, and so brought up the little girl as a Mahometan too. Thus she lived till she was sixteen years old, and there all at once came into her mind, that she knew not how or why, that she was a sinner and needed salvation. She was in great distress of mind, and went to her kind mistress for comfort, but she could not tell her of a Saviour; all the lady could do was to try to amuse her, and make her forget her trouble; she hired rope-dancers, jugglers, and serpent-charmers, and tried all the sports of which the natives of India are fond, to give her pleasure. These were of no use, and the girl remained as miserable as ever. Her mistress, deeply grieved at the distress of one whom she loved dearly, next sent for a Mahometan priest. But he had never felt the need of a Saviour, and he could not understand the girl's distress; however he took her under his care and did his best. He taught her a long string of prayers in Arabic, a language that she did not understand. She learned the long, hard words, which had no meaning to her, and she repeated them five times a day; and each time she repeated them she turned toward Mecca, the birthplace of Mahomet, and bowed her face to the ground.

Did the poor girl find comfort in these dark words and idle ceremonies? No; she felt there was no forgiveness and no salvation in these. When she had tried these prayers for three long years, the thought struck her that perhaps all the sorrow of mind was a punishment for having left the faith of her fathers, and become a Mahometan. She sent out directly in search of a Brahmin or Hindu priest, and entreated him to receive her back into the Hindu church. How do you think the

Brahmin answered her? He cursed her in the name of his god. She told him how unhappy she was, and how long she had suffered, and begged him to pity her, but he would not listen. She offered him a large sum of money, and then he was ready to do anything; so she put herself under his direction, and went again and again to him. He told her to make an offering of flowers and fruit, morning and evening, to a certain goddess who was some ways off, and once a week to offer a kid of the goats as a bloody sacrifice. In India, the people have a language of flowers; each flower means something; and when you go into a temple, and see the flowers which have been laid on the altar, you may often tell what petitions have been offered. The flowers she brought as her offering signified a bleeding heart. Oh, there was One who would not have refused such an offering! He only could have healed her broken heart, but she knew Him not. For a long, long time did she carry flowers, morning and evening, and once a week offered a kid of the goats, and sprinkled the blood on herself, and on the altar; but she found that "the blood of goats could not take away her sins," and very often she cried out in her deep distress, "Oh! I shall die, and what shall I do if I die without obtaining salvation?"

At last she became ill through the distress of her mind, and her mistress, with deep sorrow, watched her beloved companion sinking into an early grave. But one day, as she sat alone in her room, thinking, longing, and weeping, a beggar came to the door and asked alms. Her heart was so full, that she spoke of her heart's desires to all whom she met, in the hope that someone might guide her. So she began talking to the beggar passionately, "Where, oh! where may I find what I want? For I shall soon die, and oh! what shall I do if I die without obtaining salvation?"

The man told her the name of a charitable institution, where once a week two thousand poor natives were supplied with rice, and before the rice was given out, some Christian teacher used to speak to them. "I have heard talk of salvation there," he said, "for they tell of one Jesus Christ who can give salvation."

"Oh, where is he? Take me to him."

The man cared nothing about this salvation himself. He thought she was mad, and was going away, but she would not suffer him to depart till he had given an answer; she dreaded lest she should miss that prize which now seemed almost within her reach.

"Well," he said, "I can tell you of a man who will lead you to Jesus," and he directed her to that part of the town where Narraput Christian lived. Who was Narraput Christian? He was once a rich and proud Brahmin, but he had given up all his riches and honours to become a humble disciple of Jesus, and he was now an assistant missionary and preacher to his countrymen. This was the man of whom the beggar spoke. The Hindu girl gave the beggar a trifle, and that very evening she set out in search of Narraput Christian, the man who would lead her to Jesus. She went from house to house and inquired of everyone she met, where Narraput Christian lived; but no one would tell her. They all knew, but they were worshippers of idols and did not choose to tell her. It grew late and dark, and she began to be afraid of being seen out at that hour. Her heart was nearly broken, for she thought she must return as she came, without obtaining salvation. She was just turning to go home, when she saw a man walking along the road; she thought she would try once more, so she asked him the same question, where Narraput Christian lived, the man who would lead her to Jesus. To her great joy he pointed her to the house, and when she reached it, she met Narraput himself coming out at the door. She fell at his feet in tears, and wringing her hands in anguish, she asked, "Oh sir, can you lead me to Jesus? Oh! take me to him; I shall die, and what shall I do if I die without obtaining salvation?"

Narraput did not receive her as the Hindu priest had done. He raised her kindly from the ground and led her into the house, where his family were at their evening meal. "My dear young friend," said he, "sit down and tell me all."

She told him her history, and as soon as she was done, she rose and said, "Now, sir, take me to Jesus; you know where he is; oh! take me to him." Ah, if Jesus had been on earth, how willingly would He have received the poor wanderer! She thought he was on earth and that she might go to him in person; but Narraput knew that though Jesus was not here, he was just as able to pity and welcome her from his mercy-throne in heaven; so he only said, "Let us pray." All knelt down; and as he prayed, the poor Hindu felt that she had found that which she had so long wanted.

~ *The Silver Cup* ~

Nearly a hundred years ago, there stood at the foot of a high mountain in the state of Maine, a comfortable-looking, two-story farmhouse. A dense forest shielded it from the cold north wind of winter, while a summer's sun cheered it with its gladdening influence. Within the house appeared even more than comfort; as the cupboard bore testimony, filled as it was with silver and glass — all of which had come from over the wide ocean. Among other things was a massive silver tankard, bearing the name of Daniel Gordon's father — an old family heirloom.

It was a bright Sunday in June that Daniel and his family were about starting off for a meeting, when a horseman was seen fast approaching the house, from a neighboring village. He had come to warn Gordon of danger. Three notorious thieves had been lurking around the place, and as Gordon's house was remote from neighbors, he feared lest that day should be selected as a favourable opportunity to rob the rich man of his valuable silver.

Daniel, who was a strict Puritan, never absented himself from divine service, so said nothing to his wife and daughter, but taking the former with him, went forward, as he supposed, in the way of duty; merely bidding his child "read her Bible, pray, and treat strangers well, if any come in my absence." With a "God bless you!" on his lips, he drove away, leaving Hetty alone with God.

For a while she strolled around the yard, listening to the singing birds, or watching the chickens, till the sun became oppressive, and she went into the house. Then she sat down by an open window to read her Bible. She was thus busily engaged, when she heard approaching footsteps, and looking up, saw three men coming up the yard.

"Oh!" thought she, "these are the strangers father thought might come today. I will be very polite to them," and running to the door she asked them to come in, adding that she was alone, as all the rest of the family had gone to meeting.

Then she brought out food from the closet, and fresh water from the well, and placed it upon the table, not forgetting the beautiful silver cup, which was always used in company.

Hetty Gordon was so occupied in making her visitors comfortable, that she did not once stop to look at her guests, or she might have trembled a little at the dark brows and surly faces of two of the strangers. She was only "doing as she would have it done unto her," and so felt easy and happy. But all the while there was one pair of eyes fixed steadily upon her; and if there had been an evil purpose in his heart, it was fast passing away under the gentle innocence of childhood.

When the three had eaten all they wished, the eldest rose, saying, "Come! Let us go."

"What, with empty pockets?"

"Yes. I'll shoot the man who dares to take a single thing from this house, where we have been treated like brothers."

Poor Hetty now began to feel alarmed; the sharp voice of one of the speakers led her to suspect that she was in bad company, and in a beseeching manner she ran up to the pleasant-looking man, and begged him to protect her, and leave the silver cup her father thought so much of. The heart of the robber was touched, and placing his hand on Hetty's fair head, he said:

"You need not be afraid; you are too good to have harm come near you! Stay quiet in the house, and be happy again."

The robbers soon went away, leaving the young child again in solitude. When the Gordons came home from meeting, how were they terrified at the danger Hetty had been placed in! So in thanksgiving they clasped her fondly in their arms, praising the good God who had watched over her.

Not many years after, the leader of the band of thieves was condemned to die. Gordon heard of it, and resolved to visit him, to tell him there was one who remembered him with gratitude, and prayed for his redemption. He found him in his dark prison, pale, wretched, and wasted away to a mere shadow, sitting with his back to the door, with his head resting on his withered hands.

"I have come to see you," said a strange but pleasant voice, "to thank you for preserving the life of my only daughter one day, and for leaving my property untouched, when you were tempted to steal it."

The prisoner looked up with a changed face, and seemed to be glad to be remembered by anyone.

"Are you the father of that little Hetty? Oh, what a good child she was! How kind she was to the evil! It was her kindness and generosity that deterred me from robbing that day. Oh, that I had learned from her to resist evil, and live for another world! Happy for her that she has been blessed with religious parents."

The Christian remained long with the wretched, condemned man, to speak of a Saviour, repentance, and eternal things. He also prayed for his soul, and left him to the mercy of a wise and just God.

Little children, though you are young, you do have *influence*. Kindness, consideration, and goodness will make many friends for you. Learn early from the blessed Bible the way to heaven, and you will be happy on earth, and happy when you die; you will pass through life, *"fearing no evil."*

~ The Deaf and Dumb Boy ~

How well this writer remembers a dear youth who came under my pastoral care in the earlier years of my ministry. The boy had never heard the sweet sound of any human voice. At the early age of seven or eight years, he had been placed under the admirable system of instruction that has been devised for deaf-mutes; and soon became well-versed in the several branches of a common English education.

He was by nature much prone to violent fits of anger; but when about fourteen years old, a great and most wonderful change took place in him. He addressed letters to his mother from his school, to inform her of his deep religious anxiety.

When he returned home in the spring, in addition to their own instruction, his parents wisely placed such books as Doddridge's "Rise nd Progress," in his hands. He spent nearly a reading it, hardly allowing himself time ther pursuit. When he had finished it, is mother, and told her that the eighed him down was gone; d was happy! From then on, he contended earnestly and successfully with his unruly temper.

He was most scrupulous and exemplary in his observance of Christian duty. He took great interest in the spiritual welfare of his brothers and sisters. On a table in his little apartment, in a retired part of the house, would be seen the book which he prized above all others – the Bible – the gilt worn off its edges, and its leaves bent here and there, all showing how much he read that holy book. Sometimes he came to the house of God, and with his quick, beaming glances seemed to say, 'Would that I could hear!' and to gratify his wish to know what was said, on occasion, the manuscript of the discourse was sent for his reading.

Frequently he came to my house, with his slate under his arm, for conversation. I soon discovered that the love of the Saviour was the subject which was most upon his mind. But a violent disease smote him; he faded with the autumn flowers about two years after he first learned of Christ. Sickness did its work in a few days. When I went to see him, he tried to make me understand that his sufferings were very great, but that his chief grief was, that he could not read the word of God. As his father, sitting by his bedside, would spell out, with his fingers, some of the promises or his favorite passages from the Bible, although his poor body was wracked with pain, his countenance expressed by smiles an inward piece, or brightened up, as if light fell on it from within the veil.

"On a November Sabbath morning, just as the bells were ringing to call the people to the house of the Lord, death set him free, summoning him to go up to a temple, not made with hands, but to enjoy a perpetual rest in the presence of God. The snows of fifteen winters have whitened the narrow mound where his body sleeps, and the birds of as many summers have sung from his headstone, or built their nest in the branches that hang over it. In a recent summer ramble, I spent a pensive hour near the spot where we laid his dust, and where I could read many familiar names of others, known and loved, who have since fallen asleep in Christ. I thought of the words, which we almost seemed to hear whispered in the bleak gusts, when we laid it there—

"Receive my clay, thou treasurer of death!
I will no more demand my tongue,
Till the gross organ, well refined,

Shall trace the boundless flight of an
        unfettered mind,
And raise an equal song."

But his ear, that never heard the sound of the gospel, nor the songs of Zion on earth, now listens to the wonders of redemption recounted in the new song; and the voice that could never listen here below to the language of praise and prayer, shall mingle with those of angels, and the spirits of the just made perfect, in raising an 'equal song.'"

The End